JEALOUSY

CANTERWOOD CREST

JEALOUSY

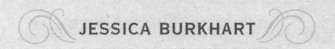
JESSICA BURKHART

ALADDIN MIX
New York London Toronto Sydney New Delhi

This book is a work of fiction. Any references to historical events, real people, or real places are used fictitiously. Other names, characters, places, and events are products of the author's imagination, and any resemblance to actual events or places or persons, living or dead, is entirely coincidental.

ALADDIN M!X

Simon & Schuster Children's Publishing Division

1230 Avenue of the Americas, New York, NY 10020

First Aladdin M!X edition February 2013

Copyright © 2013 by Jessica Burkhart

All rights reserved, including the right of reproduction

in whole or in part in any form.

ALADDIN is a trademark of Simon & Schuster, Inc., and related logo

is a registered trademark of Simon & Schuster, Inc.

ALADDIN M!X and related logo are registered trademarks

of Simon & Schuster, Inc.

For information about special discounts for bulk purchases,

please contact Simon & Schuster Special Sales

at 1-866-506-1949 or business@simonandschuster.com.

The Simon & Schuster Speakers Bureau can bring authors to your live event.

For more information or to book an event contact

the Simon & Schuster Speakers Bureau at 1-866-248-3049

or visit our website at www.simonspeakers.com.

Designed by Jessica Handelman

The text of this book was set in Venetian 301 BT.

Manufactured in the United States of America 0113 OFF

2 4 6 8 10 9 7 5 3 1

Library of Congress Control Number 2012942888

ISBN 978-1-4424-3657-2

ISBN 978-1-4424-3658-9 (eBook)

*This one's for you, Matthew, for e-mailing
and saying you're the #2 guy fan (after Drew)
and telling me about your horse, Mario!*

ACKNOWLEDGMENTS

Monica Stevenson and crew, thank you for creating one of my favorite covers! Models, you brought Lauren, Clare, and Brielle to life on the cover and looked fab doing it!

I have to throw sparkles and ♥s to everyone on Team Canterwood. A very sad event occurred while writing this book, and I've never, ever felt more support in my life. You gave Kate and me tremendous comfort when our precious cat Bailey passed away. RIP Bailey. Thank you for always listening to my drafts and giving me an um-that's-a-horrible-idea look when I came up with a plot idea that really was awful. I love you.

Canterwood wouldn't be here without everyone at Simon & Schuster's Aladdin imprint. Thank you to Alyson Heller for all of your help—you're so appreciated. Hugs to Fiona Simpson for being there professionally and personally. Thanks to Mara Anastas, Bethany Buck, Jessica Handelman (you rocked this cover!), Annie Berger, Craig Adams, Courtney Sanks, Katherine Devendorf, Nicole Russo, and Carolyn Swerdloff.

Zaffie Chandler, thank you for partnering with me for this book and allowing Sock Dreams to be written into *Jealousy*. I have sock envy of Lauren and Khloe's shopping cart! ☺

Bri Ahearn, you never miss a text or phone call. ♥

Lauren Barnholdt, you're definitely my long-lost sister. We need to schedule some serious Barnhart time!

Alex Penfold, thank you for being there.

Ross Angelella, I did *not* like you dancing in front of me to wake me up. However, I loved the marathon writing sessions and all-nighters. You kept me supplied with the best candy and provided amazing company at 3 a.m. when I was ready to call it a night.

Kate Angelella, your edits for this book, like those before it, are the only reason CC exists. I love brainstorming the latest plot with you. Even though you're in tremendous physical pain, you never let it show when you help me. You're a truly selfless best friend, and I am so lucky to have you on my writing team, let alone in my life. As we wind to a close with Canterwood, I'm going to savor every moment of writing the final two books and working with you. ♥♥♥

JEALOUSY

TRICK

I STARED INTO FAMILIAR GREEN EYES. EYES that I now could tell weren't ocean blue. The clouds had shifted past the full Halloween-night moon and, mask now in his hands, the wrong guy stood in front of me. Wrong as in my ex-boyfriend.

I reached out and shoved his chest with both hands. Taylor Frost staggered backward a step, clutching his white mask and holding up a hand. The door to the ball-room opened as more people went inside. Music blared until the doors closed.

I'd been dreaming about tonight—waking every morning with a silly grin on my face just thinking that my birthday wish might come true. That Drew Adams, my crush, would kiss me on my birthday. But I had kissed someone else and not even realized it until it was too late. How could I not have *known*?

"Lauren, I'm sorry," Taylor said. "I shouldn't have—"

I was lost in a swirl of thoughts centered on Drew: How was I going to explain this to him? Who made a mistake like this? Would I lose Drew?

I closed my eyes for a second, screaming at the thoughts to evaporate. I had to pull myself together and focus on Taylor first.

"Stop!" I hissed. "I am *not* going to let this ruin my birthday party—the one that my friends worked so hard on and *you* just crashed."

Taylor's head jerked back a fraction.

"If you want to talk, we're not doing it here," I finished.

I turned away from him, stepped around the dark-brown carriage that was covered in twinkly lights. When I'd seen the carriage, I'd imagined it taking Drew and me down the trail that Lexa had decorated and described as "romantic *and* spooky." The next carriage ride might be taking Taylor to Union.

I walked to a bench that was far enough away from my Halloween-slash-birthday masquerade party. I closed my eyes, rubbing my temples and probably ruining my makeup. Khloe's surprise—a professional makeup artist for us—felt as if it had happened days instead of mere hours ago. Khloe, Cole, and all of my other friends were inside dancing, eating, and playing games.

It felt as if I'd seen everyone but Drew tonight. I crossed my fingers that he was inside and hadn't bailed. It *was* a confusing scene, thanks to the masks. I hurried, hoping Drew or anyone else wouldn't see me leaving with a guy. More than anything, I hoped Drew hadn't witnessed The Kiss.

I shivered in the chilly late-October air as Taylor approached the bench. My light-pink dress with spaghetti straps didn't offer much warmth. I bit the inside of my cheek, trying not to let Taylor see that I was cold—it felt weak. We'd known each other for almost two years, and I'd never been this upset with him. Maybe not with anyone. My teeth chattered, betraying me.

"Even though you're mad, please take my coat," he said.

Without a word Taylor slipped off his jacket and held it out.

"Fine," I said, my tone as cold as I felt. "Thank you."

I took the black suit jacket from him and slipped it on. I'd never felt so many things at once.

Anger.

Confusion.

And . . . happiness? I had to be confusing serious fury with happiness, because there was *no* reason, not even the tiniest one, for me to be happy right now.

Taylor perched at the opposite edge of the bench and turned to me. We just looked at each other. He hadn't changed since I'd seen him only a few short months ago. His cropped blond hair was still bleached from swimming, and his tan and few freckles had faded a little. It was almost like a dream—a very *strange* dream.

"*What* are you doing here?" I asked. The words exploded from my mouth. "You're not a student! How did you get on campus? Why didn't you tell me you were coming to my birthday party? Do Ana and Brielle know? Why did you *kiss* me? Why? We're broken up! You can't show up at my school and do that!"

I stopped, realizing that I was yelling. I didn't want any attention drawn to us. I needed to talk to Taylor before any of my friends found out.

Taylor rubbed the back of his neck—something he did when he was nervous. "Lauren, again, I am *so* sorry," he said. "I had this idea that it would be a huge surprise to show up on your birthday. I missed you."

His last sentence caught me off guard and forced me to take a breath before responding.

"I missed you, too," I said, my tone still clipped. "That doesn't mean I'd ever crash a dance at Yates and kiss you. Taylor . . ." I shook my head.

"I shouldn't have done that," Taylor said. "You're right—we're broken up and I didn't consider your feelings at all. I should have talked to you about it first."

"I really wish you had—we're *friends.* I'm not your girlfriend. You know you should have talked to me before showing up here."

I rubbed my forehead. A headache was forming over my temples. I thought of Drew. Drew Adams—the *très* cute rider and guy I'd been going out with. I'd wished on every star in the sky that Drew would kiss me for the first time tonight. Now I was sitting in the cold with Taylor.

Tay and I'd had the best breakup possible after dating for five months. We'd managed to stay friends. He wasn't a *friend* like Ana or Brielle—my friends from home. As if I'd talk to him about boys! Way too weird. We'd never talked about our current relationship statuses, so he knew zero about Drew.

Taylor paused. He ran a hand over his hair. I could still smell the faintest hint of chlorine from his endless hours in the pool. "We are friends. But, Laur, I came here to see if there's a chance that we could be more than that."

The hopeful look on his face made my stomach hurt a little.

"Taylor, why are you doing this?" I asked. "You're at Yates. I'm at Canterwood. We *both* agreed on breaking up and fresh starts for both of us. Long distance isn't something either of us wanted. Want. And I . . ." I shifted on the bench.

Apparently, my birthday was going to have celebration *and* confession. Mine was going to hurt Taylor, but I couldn't let him think we had a chance at getting back together. I hated that I was about to hurt him—no matter how mad I was.

"Laur?" Taylor asked.

"Taylor, I'm sorry. You deserve to hear the truth from me. I like someone here. We've been on a few dates, and I want to keep getting to know him."

I half closed my eyes, staring at him. Taylor didn't say a word, but I knew him well. Too well for him to hide the shock, sadness, and disappointment on his face.

Finally he nodded. "Timing, huh? I'm sorry, Lauren. You're a great girl. I shouldn't have been surprised by what you told me."

I blushed. "You're being really sweet about this."

"You're too modest. I let you go. That was my mistake."

"I'm sorry," I said in a whisper. "I mean, I know we weren't together, so I didn't do anything wrong. But I'm just . . . sorry."

Taylor shook his head. "I'm not mad at you. I mean . . . jealous, yeah. I'm not going to lie. But we were broken up."

"Are," I corrected. "We *are* broken up."

"*Are* broken up," Taylor repeated. "Laur . . . are you that into this guy? You know we're good together."

"Excuse *you*?" I huffed. "Please don't ask me stuff like that. Who I'm 'into' is my choice."

Taylor was acting so *not* Taylor.

"Am I speaking in French and not realizing it?" I continued. "We talked about *all* of this before. No. Long. Distance. Nothing's different—so why are you asking me?"

The streetlamp cast light that made the silver and pink sequins sparkle on my dress as I stood, leaving my mask on the bench. I was too frustrated to sit. I glanced at the ballroom and wished that I was inside and dancing with my friends. If only Taylor had come *just* to surprise me by being here as a friend.

"Things have changed," Taylor said. He stood and looked into my eyes. "It wouldn't be long distance."

My head snapped in his direction. Words wouldn't

come out. My brain felt as though it was stuffed with the insides of the pumpkins Jill and Lex had scraped out to make jack-o'-lanterns.

"What are you talking about?" My voice shook.

"Lauren, I got accepted to Canterwood."

2

THREE WEEKS OF LIES

THERE WAS NO WAY I'D HEARD TAYLOR RIGHT.
My ears really were stuffed with pumpkin!

"*What* did you say?" I asked.

"I transferred to Canterwood."

The entire world seemed to freeze for a second. I couldn't hear, see clearly, speak, or move.

Then I felt anger. Anger so much stronger than when Taylor had kissed me. I crossed my arms. This could *not* be happening. Five seconds ago I thought that I'd talk through this kissing disaster with Taylor, his mom or dad would pick him up, and he'd go back to Union. Everything would return to normal—Tay and I both happy being friends.

He wasn't going home. He wasn't going back to Yates. Canterwood was Taylor's home now.

Our home.

Seeing Taylor, The Kiss, his confession, and this news was almost too much at once. My brain was heading toward an overload.

"Lauren?" Taylor asked, his tone tentative. He shuffled his feet but didn't come closer.

"I. Am. So. Confused." I took a few breaths. "You came to my party. You kissed me. You're not leaving. This was all planned and I knew *nothing*."

The worst part? I'd left it out.

A small piece of me was glad to see him. *That* confused me the most. I didn't want to be happy, not after everything he'd done tonight, but Taylor was familiar and comforting no matter how much I didn't want it in this moment. I had a Union ally at Canterwood now. But I wasn't saying that to Taylor. Not tonight, anyway.

"You're a student *here*?" I had to ask again.

"Yes."

"Since when? Taylor, if you really thought of us as friends, why didn't you tell me?" I turned in a circle, fighting the urge to scream. "Do you have any idea what this feels like? Do you?"

Taylor looked down, then back up at me. "I did everything the wrong way. I ambushed you and kept a big secret from you. This wasn't how I envisioned tonight."

I stood—silent. There had to be more.

"I don't want to make excuses. I just want to tell the truth."

I kept standing—waiting.

"I wasn't happy at Yates," Taylor said. "I'm not trying to make this an oh-poor-Taylor thing. My dad was driving me insane. Remember his threats about pulling me off the swim team?"

"They got worse?" My heart twisted a little. Mr. Frost had always been a stress on Taylor. He had laserlike focus on grooming Taylor to take over Frost Investments. Taylor didn't want it, but the harder Tay pushed, the more Mr. Frost insisted.

"We fought all of the time, and I knew I had to get out," Taylor continued. "I looked for boarding schools with swim teams. Academics that would impress my dad. Schools with business classes as extracurriculars."

"And Canterwood came up how?"

"I swear, I looked all over the East Coast. Not one other school had everything that Canterwood did. Plus, it was close enough to home that I could easily get to Union for the summers and promise Dad to be in his office every day."

"And your parents agreed? Just like that?" I asked. "I can't believe it."

Taylor exhaled. "Me either. Dad took a week to look through everything about Canterwood. He and my mom talked a lot. They spoke to the headmistress, and Dad called a dozen Canterwood graduates."

"How did they tell you?"

"We sat down for dinner on a night Dad was home on time, and he and my mom told me that I could go if I was accepted."

"When?" I asked.

"About three weeks ago." Again Taylor ran his hand over his hair.

I threw up my arms, holding both palms upward. "*Three* weeks ago?"

"I wanted to tell you," Taylor said. "You were the first person that I wanted to call, Laur. I promise. I was afraid at every step. At first I thought there was no way my dad would say yes. Then when he did, I was convinced because it was mid-semester that I wouldn't get in. It took two weeks for me to get an answer."

"And then?"

"*And* when I did get my acceptance letter, I wasn't sure Dad would keep his promise, until he dropped me off."

"So, you lied for two weeks while you waited for an answer. Then you lied for another week after you got in. Nice, Taylor."

I regretted my words immediately. Taylor's cheeks went pink. *You can be mad, but you don't have to be mean*, I said to myself.

"Sorry," I murmured. "I understand why you were scared."

Taylor took a step toward me. He reached out with his left arm, as if he was going to touch my arm, but pulled his arm back, holding his mask with both hands. Even under the dim light the desperation in his eyes was visible.

"You're the last one who should apologize," he said. "This day—*your* day—wasn't supposed to be like this. If I could do it over, I would have called you the second that I decided to apply. You would have been there for me."

"Tay, I'm happy for you—so happy—that you got away from your dad," I said. "You know I am. But I'm mad, too! And confused. You're here. At my school. The place where I came for a fresh start."

Taylor's eyes went to the tiny pebbles below our feet that surrounded the bench. His shoulders slumped a little.

"It's not that I don't want you here," I said quickly. "It's just going to take me a little bit of time to adjust. You understand, right?"

He raised his eyes to mine. "Absolutely. I know the last

thing you ever expected was for someone from your old school to enroll here. I can't even imagine how weird that must feel."

I blew out a breath that was visible in the cold air, and sat back down. "Thank you for everything you told me," I said. "I know you—you would never intentionally hurt me. I don't want to hurt you, either, but we're not getting back together. I want to still be friends and enjoy experiencing Canterwood together."

Taylor sat too, his body turned toward mine. "Really just friends?"

"Yes." I visualized Drew's face and knew I owed it to him and Taylor to be honest.

A look crossed Taylor's face like he wanted to say something. Instead he pressed his lips together.

"I hate that *your* first night at Canterwood came with news like this," I said. "I don't want to lead you on."

"You didn't have to be honest—not after I lied to you." Taylor slumped a little. "I shouldn't have kissed you and just assumed . . ."

"Yeah. Because I have to go find him and explain now," I said.

"I'm sorry. He shouldn't be mad at you—it was my fault." Taylor paused, playing with his mask. "If you need me to do anything, I will. Even though . . ."

I gave him a few seconds, but he sat still and quiet. "Even though what?" I asked.

Taylor sighed and shrugged one shoulder. "Even though it would be hard."

Argh. The last thing I wanted was for Drew and Taylor to have issues with each other.

"Thanks, but I'll handle it. I don't want to go around in circles all night. It's your first night here. That's special too. Can we talk—really talk—when we're not sitting outside freezing?"

"Of course, and I didn't mean to keep you away from your party for so long. I've messed up so much tonight."

"Lucky that you're sticking around in case I need you to fix anything." I smiled at him, and Tay smiled back.

"I want our relationship to stay like it was—mature—and not be tarnished because of my stupidity tonight," Taylor said.

That was Taylor. Even when we weren't together, he liked me enough that he always—well, almost always—carefully considered my feelings. He had what my dad called an "old soul."

"One mistake didn't ruin everything," I said. "We'll figure this out."

"You asked about Bri and Ana earlier," he said. "They didn't know until my last day at Yates. I asked them to let me tell you myself. Don't be mad at them—they only kept it a secret because I begged them to."

I wondered if that had anything to do with the disconnect among Brielle, Ana, and me lately. Maybe they'd been trying to stay off Skype on purpose because they were afraid they'd spill Taylor's secret.

"I don't want to be mad at anyone, but I *do* want to go inside."

"Laur?"

"Yeah?" I stood, smoothing my dress and picking up my mask.

"This guy better be *really* good to you."

"He is."

It was too weird talking to Taylor about Drew. I thought I'd have until Thanksgiving or Christmas break to tell Tay about my new guy. *If* Drew and I kept going in that direction. Right now I wanted to cease all boy talk and go. I looked away from Taylor and at the ballroom.

As if on cue, the ballroom doors opened. Lexa, Clare, and Khloe stepped outside. Their hand masks were at their sides. Each girl looked in a different direction.

Whew. Perfect timing, guys, I thought.

3

TOMORROW.
THE NEXT DAY.
THE DAY AFTER THAT.

I TIPPED MY CHIN TOWARD THE DOORS.
Taylor followed my gaze.

"Those are my friends," I said. "They are probably about to post a missing persons report."

"Then we better hurry," Tay said. Together we started back to my party.

"Do you have a dorm room?" I asked. I'd wanted our talk to end when we'd left the bench, but now I had so many things to ask Taylor. "When did you even get here? What about your stuff?"

Then I *laughed*. It was as if my body didn't know how else to react. "I have so many questions. Too many to ask before we get to my friends."

Taylor grinned, and the tension in my neck and

shoulders seemed to slowly loosen. If I closed my eyes, I could almost pretend that Tay and I were friends walking out of a movie or leaving the gym back in Union.

"Maybe I can BBM you tomorrow and we can meet up to talk?" Taylor asked.

"Sure. But where? When? And how?" I asked, referring to my questions from eons ago. Taylor knew me well enough not to need more explanation than that.

"Where: Wren Hall. When: Got here a couple of hours ago. How: I brought what I needed for tonight, and the movers are bringing my stuff tomorrow."

"I haven't been by Wren," I said. "But I know it's close to The Slice. Did you meet your roommate or *anything*?"

I let out a tiny breath of relief that Taylor was in Wren and not Blackwell—Drew's dorm hall.

Taylor shook his head. "Nope. He wasn't in our room and I wasn't there long. All I know about him is that his name is Matthew. My dorm monitor, Ben, is a super-chill guy. I explained that it was a friend's birthday and I really wanted to surprise her at her party. He was cool about it. As long as I was back by curfew and met him tomorrow for an orientation briefing, I could go."

"Did you get lost? I probably would have ended up

in the woods, especially since it's dark out." My chatter helped distract me from my nerves.

We were almost at the ballroom. Lexa, Khloe, and Clare hadn't spotted us yet. They still craned their necks and stood on tiptoes looking for me.

"Nah, I looked at the campus map a couple of times before tonight," Taylor said. "I'm going to wander around tomorrow and check out everything."

Tomorrow. Taylor was going to be here tomorrow. And the next day.

"You should definitely BBM me," I said.

Just because I was into Drew didn't mean I couldn't be around Tay. Especially since we'd been friends all along. Drew would understand . . . *right*?

"Um, after the movers and stuff, you know," I finished. "Talking would be a good idea."

"Sounds good," Taylor said.

I glued my eyes on my friends. Lexa glanced in my direction, and I lifted a hand. She took a step forward, waved back, and said something to Khloe and Clare. Khloe held out her arm, putting her palm up in a *what's going on?* gesture. Clare put her lips close to Khloe's ear and must have whispered something that made Khloe's arm fall to her side.

It was hard to tell if my friends were staring at Taylor or at me. I wasn't close enough to see their expressions clearly, but I *knew* they didn't recognize Taylor. It was as if the landing was an island. If they went down the stairs and came toward me, they'd be swallowed up by the sea.

Out of the corner of my eye, I watched Tay for a few seconds. Everything about him screamed *relaxed*, from his dropped shoulders to the easy swing in his walk.

We reached a split in the sidewalk. Part of the sidewalk continued to the ballroom. The other started toward the north side of the campus.

Light streamed from every window of the enormous ballroom. Now we were close enough to hear lyrics of a pop song. The horse and carriage were gone—someone was out on the trail that Lexa had decorated. I went to the right and walked a few steps before turning back to see that Taylor had stopped.

He smiled at me. "I hope I didn't ruin the rest of your night. Have fun, okay? We'll talk tomorrow."

"You're going back to Wren? Now?"

The second the question had left my mouth, I heard how dumb it sounded. Of course he was headed to Wren Hall. He *lived* there now. I'd just yelled at him for crashing my party, and it wasn't Taylor's style to be a repeat offender. But this was my birthday and Taylor was here. Even though he'd come for the wrong reasons, I'd be a bad friend to let Taylor go and not ask if he wanted to come to my party.

Taylor tilted his head, eyeing something behind me, then focusing on me. "I'm glad the three girls staring at us are your friends and not your enemies," he said. "They look *pretty* intense."

I grinned. "'Intense' is the right word, and yes, they would be scary enemies. I'd be holed up in my room hiding."

Tay laughed. "So would I! And yeah, I'm going back to my room. Maybe my roommate will be there. I can at least unpack what I brought."

We both paused. I could feel my friends' stares at the back of my head, and the question I was about to ask made my heart pound so hard.

4

PARTY CRASHER TURNED GUEST

"TAYLOR . . . DO YOU WANT TO COME TO MY party?" I asked.

"Oh, Laur, I—"

"I know what I said before," I interjected, cutting him off. "I'm still mad at you for kissing me. You *are* a student here, though, and all of my friends are inside."

"Laur, no, I can't. You're way too generous after what I did tonight. You'll already have to explain me to your friends, and I don't want to take any more attention away from you. It's your birthday."

"You're right," I said. "It is *my* birthday, and I'd really like it if you came to my party." I smiled. "C'mon. If you say no, I'll send my posse after you."

That made Taylor smile. "I definitely don't want those

girls coming after me." He shifted and tugged at the sleeves of his crisp white shirt. "Okay. I'd really like to come as a guest and not a crasher."

Taylor fell into step next to me as we walked toward the ballroom. There was no way I would have felt right if he'd gone back to his room. But now I had goose bumps from nerves. Drew was (hopefully!) inside, and I was about to walk back into my party with my ex-boyfriend. My new crush wasn't even my *current* boyfriend, and tonight he'd meet Tay.

Doubt settled into my stomach, making me feel seasick. I'd only known Drew for a couple of months. What if he disagreed with my decision to invite Taylor? I wasn't going to stop being Taylor's friend if Drew had a problem with it. But Drew didn't seem like *that* kind of guy. I wanted to make the right choices for everyone. Most of all, I didn't want to lose Drew. Almost every girl in my grade had a crush on him, and it wasn't just because he was cute. There were so many things that I liked about Drew—I'd get lost making a list in my head. I'd already made my intentions clear to Taylor, so I had to find Drew ASAP and talk to him.

I shook off my thoughts, and my eyes connected with Khloe's first. Her own were wide, and she wasn't blinking.

Clare and Lex smiled as Tay and I approached them. My friends were dressed in the most elegant and gorgeous dresses, and, arms at their sides, they each held a decorated stick attached to a beautiful mask.

Choosing our dresses and accessories had been no easy task. The memory of shopping online at Macy's made me smile. Khloe and I had gotten so into it, we'd even sent Clare, Lex, and Jill links to dresses that we thought they might like.

Khloe looked sophisticated in her strapless black dress with a satin belt that tied in the front. Closest to her, Lexa's tangerine dress with floral appliqué complemented her mocha-colored skin. My favorite detail of Lex's sleeveless dress was the bodice—each flower had a tiny pearl in the center. Clare's amethyst-colored dress made her long red hair pop. Almost out of stock on Macy's Website, the capped-sleeve dress was pleated and had a tulle underlay. Looking at each of them in their dresses and holding their masks calmed my nerves a little. These were my new friends, and I was about to introduce them to one of my old friends.

Taylor and I stopped at the bottom of the stairs. *Taylor, welcome to Canterwood*, I thought.

5

CUTIES IN CAULDRONS

I SMILED UP AT MY FRIENDS, TAKING A QUICK breath.

"I stepped out for a breath of fresh air and came back with a friend from home," I said. "Is that a crazy birthday present or what?"

The girls giggled, but I could see their *get to the truth already!* looks.

"That's quite the surprise present!" Clare said. "I hope one of my friends from home just appears when I turn thirteen. Or maybe stuff like that only happens to people who have birthdays on Halloween."

"I think that's it," I said, trying to keep a serious look on my face. "When this cauldron popped up on the lawn and this guy next to me stepped out, I thought, 'Whoa! You guys *really* went all out!'"

"That cauldron better still be there," Lexa said. She grinned. "I need a cute boy to pop up out of nowhere!"

We all laughed.

"Guys," I said. "This is Taylor Frost. He's a friend from home. No cauldron involved with his appearance, though. Sorry, Lexa."

Lex stuck out her lower lip. "Boo."

"Oh. *Oh*," Khloe said. Her blond hair shimmered under the lights as she shook her head. She put both hands on her hips and grinned. Her near-palpable excitement almost sent sparks into the air. "Taylor! Taylor Frost! At Lauren's party! Omigod!"

Uh-oh! I thought. *Khloe's going to freeeak out!*

"Taylor, hi," Lexa said, stepping in front of Khloe.

I shot her a quick, grateful smile, and Lexa winked back. She knew that when Khloe got excited, the girl got *excited*. I'd told Khlo everything about the Taylor saga. If no one stepped in and gave Khloe a moment to compose herself, my roommate would bury Taylor under a zillion rapid-fire questions.

"I'm Lexa Reed," Lex said. "This is Clare Bryant . . ."

Clare smiled. "Hey, nice to meet you, Taylor."

". . . and Khloe Kinsella," Lex added.

"Hi!" Khloe said. "Lauren's told you that I'm her awful roommate who plays emo music twenty-four/seven, fills our fridge with kelp smoothies, and snores, right?"

Taylor looked at me, then at Khloe. He had the deer-in-the-headlights look.

"No, not at all," Taylor said, shaking his head. "Lauren's never said any of that."

Khloe! I yelled at her in my head. She'd scared Taylor—just like she'd done to me when we had first met.

"Khloe's an actress," I said, jumping in. "She—"

"She likes you from everything Lauren's said and was just teasing," Khlo said. She dropped her act. "It's really nice to meet you."

Taylor smiled at her—the kind of smile that I knew meant he liked Khloe's sense of humor now that he was in on the joke.

"It's cool to meet all of you," Taylor said. "Lauren's mentioned you guys before. Actually, she *did* mention that her roommate snores. . . ." Taylor looked at Khloe, a teasing gleam in his eyes.

Khloe's jaw dropped, and she covered her open mouth with her hand. I winked and stuck out my tongue at her.

"Lauren's mentioned you, too," Clare said. "We thought

we had planned *every* surprise for tonight, but you coming here from Union is def the biggest one of all!"

"You *did* come a long way for LT," Khloe said. She played with the ostrich plume on her white satin mask. "We totes know you're her ex!" she blurted out.

I looked at Khloe sideways. *Khloe!* I mouthed.

Khloe's face reddened. "But we know you're not a *bad* ex!" she added. "We know it was mutual. The breakup, I mean."

Oh my God! I'm going to kill Khloe! I thought. After everything Taylor had told me back at the bench, Khloe had no idea that my breakup was now a teensy bit more complicated.

Clare played with a lock of her red hair, and Lexa inspected her mask. I half expected Taylor to excuse himself, run to Wren Hall, and never come within ten feet of me or my friends again.

Khloe stepped out from behind Lexa and made eye contact with me. She curtsied. "I hope you all will congratulate me on making this the most awkward introduction in history to occur on Canterwood Crest Academy grounds. Not since the school was founded in nineteen . . ." She frowned. "Nineteen whatever—just way before cell phones and anything cool had been invented."

I couldn't stop myself from smiling. Beside me Taylor did the same.

"My words that have surely embarrassed Lauren's friend, the seemingly nice Taylor Frost, should be included in the student handbook under a new section: Improper Methods of Introduction. I hope this night, October thirty-first, is remembered not just for Lauren's birthday or Halloween but for how I welcomed a visitor to our campus."

Lexa nodded, making a serious face and patting Khloe's arm. *They are going to drag me away for questioning when I tell them that Taylor's a Canterwood student now!* I thought.

"Please make sure to take this story to the yearbook staff," Khloe continued. "I must be recognized as 'The Seventh Grader Who Blurted Out Embarrassing Things,' along with my other most honorable accolades."

Khloe bowed her head and took a step back.

Silence.

Slowly Khloe lifted her head as if she was peeking at us to see if I was going to forgive her or revoke her invite to my party.

We all burst into laughter.

"I know I told you Khlo was an actress," I said to Taylor. "I left out how *good* of an actress she really is."

Taylor and Khloe traded smiles.

I went from wanting to shake KK to applauding her for being the best icebreaker. Her methods weren't conventional, but they worked.

"Taylor did come to surprise me for my birthday," I said. "He had another surprise too."

Lex, Clare, and Khloe raised their eyebrows.

"Do tell!" Khloe said, leaning on the iron railing.

"Like I said, Taylor's a friend from home," I said. "He used to attend Yates."

"Wait," Clare said. She frowned. "You said 'used to.'"

I wasn't going to embarrass Taylor with the truth about his father. He would have plenty of time to decide whom to tell and when.

"He's not at Yates anymore," I continued, twirling my mask in my hand. "It wasn't the right fit for him, and he decided to transfer."

"Oh, cool," Lexa said. "What school? Is it close to us?"

"About as close as you can get," I said. "Taylor was just accepted to Canterwood. It's his first night on campus."

6

THE COVER-UP

"OMIGOD!" LEXA, CLARE, AND KHLOE SAID at the same time.

"Sorry. I mean, welcome!" Clare said, recovering first.

"I'm glad you found a school that you liked," Lexa said. "It's great that you have a friend to help you settle in."

"Omigod!" Khloe said again. "Sorry! It's just . . . *wow*. You're a student. Here. At Canterwood."

Taylor smiled at everyone. He was being great with my friends. "Crazy how it worked out," he said. "I'm still kind of in shock too."

"How about we go inside, grab snacks and drinks, and chat more?" I suggested. "Maybe find a quiet-ish place so we don't throw Taylor into the middle of a party at a new school?"

"If I were you, I'd be a little overwhelmed," Clare said to Taylor. There was a look of understanding in her blue eyes. "Promise not to introduce you to every single one of my friends tonight."

Lexa and Khloe added their agreement.

Taylor and I went up the stairs, following my friends inside. Tay slowed as his eyes wandered around the giant room.

"Wow," he said. "*This* is a party."

Fog curled out of the machine Khloe had borrowed from the theater department, and mist covered the floor and added a spooky feel. Tables of all shapes and sizes were positioned around the room, and there was plenty of space in the middle for dancing. I knew Jill had been on table duty, and she'd nailed it. Every table was draped with a silver, purple, or black fabric. A pumpkin that fit the table size had a freshly carved face and a flickering votive inside. Benches with soft, cushioned black leather had been lined up along the wall for extra seating.

As if that wasn't enough to look at, everyone had stuck to Khloe's dress code. Or . . . maybe she'd tossed them at the door if someone hadn't followed her "request," aka "command," to dress up.

Girls swayed to music in strapless, sleeveless, capped-sleeve, bubble, bandage, and every other type dress, and the variety of dress colors formed a kind of rainbow across the floor.

"Aren't the masks the most beautiful part?" I asked Taylor.

"I've never seen anything like these. I was thinking Mardi Gras masks, but these are *serious*. They are so ornate and detailed."

I nodded. "I did a lot of looking online. Some have ostrich plumes, some have rooster feathers—it all depends on what you want."

"Let me see yours up close."

I handed Taylor the stick of my mask. His thumb brushed my pinky when he grasped it. Months ago that would have made me shiver and do a Taylor-touched-my-hand cartwheel in my head.

This time? Nothing. Just our fingers touching for a half second on the braided silver fabric that covered the stick.

Taylor gingerly held my mask. "It's so you, LT. I couldn't see well enough in the moonlight. It's pretty."

I beamed. "Thanks!"

It had taken me *hours* to find the Venetian-style mask. It was the lightest silver with tiny pink rhinestones in random swirls and matching rosy pink around the eyes. Silver trimmed the mask's edge, and on the side an oval-shaped crystal jewel hid the tips of the dozen whimsical, thin feathers that fanned to the outside of the mask. Taylor handed it back to me.

"Your masks are great too," he said to my friends. He nodded at Lexa, Clare, and Khloe while looking over their masks.

I *almost* looped my arm through his. I was so excited about how well he was getting along with my friends. Each of them smiled, holding out their mask so Taylor could see.

Khloe's mask was shiny white satin on a matching stick. On the right side a quarter-size rhinestone drew attention to an ostrich plume that was at least a foot long. Smaller feathers formed a half circle on the mask's side.

Lexa offered Taylor her mask, and he took it and held it up to his face.

"Does this match my skin tone?" Taylor asked, batting his eyes.

Any worries I had about Taylor at Canterwood were gone. He felt like a Canterwood student, my friends seemed to like him, and I was excited to show him around

JEALOUSY

campus tomorrow. Taylor just had a certain ease about him that made him fit in anywhere.

"Totally," Lexa managed to say through her laughter. Clare, Khloe, and I were still giggling.

Taylor handed the shimmery black mask dotted with tiny pearls back to Lex. One of my favorite details of Lex's *très* chic find were angel-hair-spaghetti-thin black wires that curled out from one side and had a cluster of pearls at their base.

"Don't forget about mine," Clare said. She held her mask up to her face. The deep purple mask had small black beads draped over it. It complemented her red hair and amethyst-colored dress.

Taylor told Clare how much he liked her mask and showed his to my friends. I couldn't have been prouder or more relieved at how well he fit in. But I *had* to find Drew. I waited for an opportunity when everyone was talking, and I made eye contact with Lexa. I held her gaze and mouthed, *Drew.*

"Let's get this night going!" Lexa said, brushing back her curls. "Khlo, can you grab us seats?" she asked.

Khloe nodded and disappeared into the crowded room of people dancing or sipping sparkling cider and pink lemonade, and groups that had clustered together to talk.

"Want to check out food and drinks with me, Taylor?" Clare asked. "We haven't cut the cake yet—well, more like eaten the birthday cupcakes, but there are so many fun appetizers."

"Thanks, Clare. I'm starving," Taylor said.

"I worked on the menu, and we've got witch's brew to drink, sugar cookies shaped like pumpkins with orange frosting, *and* peeled grapes if you're in the mood for eyeballs."

"I'm *always* craving eyeballs! Lead the way."

Taylor followed Clare into the mix of people and toward the refreshments tables.

As they walked away, Clare turned her head around, giving me a quick wink.

"What was that for?" I asked Lexa, who was still beside me.

"Come over here!" Lexa tugged on my arm, practically dragging me into an empty corner of the ballroom. I almost had to jog to keep up with her.

"Oh my God, Lex!" I said as we stopped along the wall. "Taylor totally ambushed me!"

"You have to tell me *everything*, but first, Drew's here and he's been looking for you."

"Drew's here? He really came!" Taylor and everything

that had just happened fled from my mind for a second as I reveled in the news that Drew was here.

Lexa waved her hand in front of my face. "You can freak out about that later. Clare and I kept covering for you."

"Oh no . . ." My excitement was replaced with nervousness.

"Drew came up to me and said he'd been looking for you all over and couldn't find you. He asked if I knew where you were. I had no clue, since I hadn't even seen you leave. I told Drew that I didn't know where you were but I'd tell you that he was looking for you."

"Lex, I'm so sorry," I said, rubbing my temples.

"I looked for you while trying *not* to seem like I was doing anything," Lexa said. She smiled at a guy from our class as he walked by. "So," she continued once the guy was gone, "I started to get worried when I couldn't find you after a while. I kept telling myself it was the masks and maybe Drew had already found you and whisked you away on a carriage ride."

"Instead I was really off talking to Taylor."

"I asked Khloe if she'd seen you, but she was dancing with Zack and they were making googly eyes at each other. Totally not helpful."

"I was gone at least half an hour," I said. "What happened after you talked to Khloe?"

Someone turned down the music, and Lexa stepped closer. "Clare found me. She told me that Drew had asked her about you and she'd lied to him."

"Lied how?"

"Clare had seen you and a guy she'd assumed was Drew go outside. But since Drew was standing in front of her and looking for you, Clare realized you'd left with another guy."

I groaned. "This is *so* bad!"

"It could have been. Clare saved you—she told Drew that a group of your friends from English class had dragged you off on a carriage ride. Perfect timing, because the carriage was actually gone."

"Did Drew *see* me outside?"

Lexa shook her head. "Don't think so. Clare wrangled Khloe away from Zack for a few minutes and told her the deal. Khlo managed to get Zack and Drew into a show-off at who was better at pool."

"So I made it back in time before—"

"Found you!"

I jumped at the voice behind me. I whirled around to see a wide-eyed, unmasked Drew.

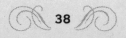

"Sorry I scared you, Lauren," he said. "Was the haunted trail ride really spooky?"

My mouth was dry. I had to tell him about Taylor, *and* my friends didn't even know the whole story.

"Yeah, Lauren got out of the carriage after the ride was over and tracked me down to say I might have gone a teensy bit overboard with the glowing-eyed bats." Lexa smiled at Drew and made a mock *you're a total wimp* face at me.

"Happy birthday," Drew said. "I got here late and then couldn't find you. I'm glad I finally did."

He took a step closer, and I could smell his body wash's hint of grapefruit.

"Me too," I said. "I'm so happy you came."

Lexa tipped her head and took a step back, smiling. "I'll see you two later."

She was gone, leaving me to tell Drew what had happened tonight.

7

YOUR WISH ISN'T COMING TRUE

I STARED INTO DREW'S EYES. THEY LOOKED shades bluer tonight—if that was even possible.

"You look beautiful," Drew said, his eyes not leaving mine. "I'm not sure what kind of dress that's called, but whatever it is—it's pretty on you."

I laughed. "Thank you, and because you complimented me, I won't take points off because you didn't know that I'm wearing a spaghetti-strap dress with a sequin bodice, and if I said the rest, you'd probably be confused for the rest of the night."

Drew twisted his mouth into an *oops* gesture. "Yeah . . . you lost me at 'spaghetti-strap.'"

"I *do* know what you're wearing," I said. "The thin blue pinstripes are great against your white shirt, and

I like the black jacket and matching pants."

Drew wiped fake sweat off his brow. "Zack and I helped each other. At least I know *one* of us looks good." He grinned. "And you haven't even seen my mask yet."

He held up a black mask with silver cross-stitching that covered his face from forehead to chin.

"I love it, but you better keep it off or we'll lose each other again," I said. "Here's mine." I put my mask up to my face, and Drew's reaction was exactly what I'd hoped for. A smile spread across his face. He took a quick breath.

"Wow," Drew said. "Lauren, that looks so cool on you."

"I'm glad you like it," I said.

I let my mind wander for a second. I wanted to stay behind my mask and dance in the ballroom.

"Want to dance?" Drew asked.

"Like you read my mind," I said. "But first, can we go somewhere quiet to talk for a sec?"

Drew nodded. His eyes lingered on me for a second. "C'mon. I know a spot."

He took my hand, and we sidestepped around clusters of people talking, dancing, and eating, until Drew stopped. He twisted an antique brass doorknob and pushed open a door that had been partially hidden by draped purple fabric.

We stepped into a dimly lit side hallway. It was narrow with brick walls on both sides. Iron-and-glass lanterns were spaced every few feet along both sides of the hall, and small bulbs emitted soft yellow light. At one end an EXIT sign glowed. The thick walls absorbed most of the music coming from the other side. I could actually hear myself think.

"Is this okay?" Drew asked. "It's heated in here, at least, or we can go outside if you want."

"This is perfect," I said. "I needed a private space to talk to you."

Drew, standing across from me, leaned his back against the brick wall. "Is everything okay?"

I was quiet. For a very long time.

"No. Not really," I said finally. "Lex, Khlo, and my other friends were covering for me tonight. Something *really* unexpected happened, and they did what best friends do. I want you to hear the whole story from me before anyone else tells you."

"You can talk to me," Drew said. "Whatever it is—I want to know."

I hope you really mean that and don't storm out of here the second I'm finished.

"I've told you a little about Taylor Frost—my ex-boyfriend," I said.

"Right. Mutual breakup."

"Yes, and tonight Taylor came here."

Drew's eyes widened. "He came to Canterwood? For your birthday?"

I chewed the inside of my cheek. "Yes and no. He came to my party to surprise me and to tell me some incredibly huge news." I looked down, not wanting to see Drew's reaction. "Taylor applied and was accepted to Canterwood."

Drew was silent for a moment. Every sound in the tiny hallway seemed amplified, and I heard both of us breathing.

"If he's here, does that mean you want to get back together?" Drew asked. There was zero emotion in his tone—it gave me no sense of what he felt.

I shook my head, bringing my eyes to Drew's. "No. No. I promise. I already told Taylor that you and I had just started something and I was *not* getting back with him."

"Were you off talking?" Drew asked. "Is that what your friends were covering?"

"Taylor and I were talking, and yes, that's why Lex and everyone covered for me. But they didn't know Taylor was coming either."

This was it. This was the moment when Drew was either going to walk away or stay with me.

"Drew, I want to tell you everything. I like you, and

I don't want to keep secrets. Taylor found me inside the ballroom, and I thought he was *you*. He had a mask covering his face and hair—I was so caught up in the party, the lighting was dim, and all I could think was 'Drew actually came to my party!'"

"Laur, of course I was coming," Drew said. "We must have been missing each other for a while inside."

I nodded. "We definitely were. When Taylor found me, he led me outside and toward a carriage. I thought my birthday wish was about to come true."

"What did you wish for?" Drew's voice was soft.

"That you would kiss me on my birthday," I said shyly, softly. "But I know that won't happen now."

"Why?"

"Because when Taylor took me outside, he kissed me. Drew, I'm so sorry!" I squeezed my eyes shut. "I thought Taylor was you until he kissed me. I knew something wasn't right, and I pushed him away." My voice bounced off the walls. "I was so furious at Taylor that *I* dragged him away from the ballroom and freaked out at him for kissing me, showing up without telling me, and just assuming he and I were getting back together."

I opened my eyes and saw that Drew had straightened, no longer leaning against the wall.

"He kissed you?" Drew's eyes were midnight blue.

I nodded.

"But you swear you don't want to be with him. Even though he's here now and you guys are—were—friends. You do not want to be with Taylor."

I clutched my mask stick so hard, I thought it would crack. "I don't. I don't want to be with Taylor. Whether he's here or at home. I want to keep going out with you."

I took a step toward him, and our faces were inches apart. He had to know everything. I didn't want to lose him.

"I really like you, Drew, and I'm so sorry I got swept up in my party. There's no excuse. If I were you, I'd be so offended that I'd even thought for a second that someone else was you."

We looked at each other. It felt as though all of the oxygen was disappearing from the hallway. There wasn't room for Drew to back up, and my feet were rooted to the ground. My knees felt like they'd give out if I moved.

"Lauren, your birthday wish isn't coming true tonight."

8

THE PIRATE AND THE HAUNTED HOUSE

I KNEW, I JUST KNEW, THAT DREW WAS GOING to break up with me. But I didn't know it would feel like *this*.

Tears made his shape blurry, and I stepped back, resting my back against the wall. I wanted Drew to just walk out the door. I'd embarrassed him enough. I wasn't going to beg him to accept my apology.

Shoes shuffled, and two cool hands touched my elbows.

"Look at me," Drew said, his voice gentle.

I gazed up at him, trying to keep my chin from wobbling.

"I'm not breaking up with you. What I meant was, I wanted to kiss you on your birthday too. It was going to be a special night for both of us. But because of . . ."

Drew swallowed. "*Taylor*, that's not how I want our first kiss to be. It'll happen on a night just for us—you and me—when *I'm* the first one to kiss you."

"You—you're not—but I—"

Drew touched my chin, making my queasy stomach a little calmer. "You didn't cause anything that happened tonight. I know you like me, and you're honest. If you had kissed Taylor and felt something, you would have told me. Or you could have kept this whole thing to yourself. But that's not *you*."

"I'd never keep anything like that from you."

"I know. You're honest, Laur, and that's part of why I like you." He smiled. "I mean, I really don't want to think about another guy kissing you. Let alone the fact that he's an ex. But it happened, and you came to me with the truth. I'd be pretty dumb and egotistical to stop seeing this girl that I like over a *really* big misunderstanding."

I raised an eyebrow and touched my pointer finger to my chin. "You like a girl? Who is she?"

Drew laughed. It was the way he laughed that I knew we were okay. His laughter reached deep down into his belly, making his shoulders shake a little. It was the type of laugh that couldn't be faked. His great laugh was one of the things I'd been drawn to when we'd met.

Drew took my hand in his and bubbles tickled my stomach.

"Ready to party, birthday girl?" he asked.

"So ready," I said. "Full disclosure—Taylor's in there. I invited him because—"

Drew squeezed my hand. "Hey, you don't have to explain that to me. I want to go inside, have fun, and make this an awesome night for you. If Taylor's the guy you've told me about, then we're not going to have a problem."

I squeezed Drew's hand back, and he reached for the doorknob. Together we stepped out of the hallway. Forcing away any lingering worries, I let Drew lead me to the dance floor.

The way Drew and I danced, there was no way I could have panicked about Taylor even if I'd wanted to. We'd been moving all over the floor. I'd learned that Drew's dance skills rivaled his riding ones.

I leaned into Drew's ear. "So thirsty," I said. "You?"

Drew nodded. "I'll get sodas. Mind grabbing snacks?"

"No prob. I'll find you in five."

We split up, and the music lowered, as did the lights. They were dim enough so the jack-o'-lanterns glowed brighter, the twinkly lights draped around the room seemed to wink at me, and the room *really* felt like Halloween.

I hadn't seen Taylor while Drew and I had danced. I'd been careful *not* to look for him too often and be rude to Drew. Khloe and Zack had swayed beside Drew and me for a couple of songs. It had been fun to dance with my friends!

Just when I'd started to worry that I hadn't seen Taylor, Lexa had given me the "okay" signal with her fingers when I'd mouthed *Taylor* to her. Instinctively I think I knew that my friends were keeping an eye on Tay and weren't going to let any more surprises occur at my party.

I smiled to myself as I grabbed a black plastic plate, thinking about how much fun I'd had on the dance floor.

I used a ladle to pour candy corn onto my plate. Next, chocolate-chip-and-marshmallow-sprinkled Chex Mix that Jill had created a couple of days ago. A ghost cookie for me. A bat cookie for Drew.

"LT!"

I popped an M&M into my mouth, looking up at Khloe. She slid to a halt in front of me. She'd come so close, I thought she'd topple us over.

"Hey! How are things going with Zack?" I asked.

Khloe smiled. "Amaze! He's perrr-fect! If we're not dancing, he's getting me a drink or snack."

I danced in place. "Yay! I'm so glad you guys are having fun. I'm getting food, and Drew's on drinks duty."

Khlo gave me a sideways look. "Tell. Me. Everything."

I nodded, making a serious face. "I will! But if I did that right now, we'd miss the rest of the party. You'll get the full report tonight—I promise."

Khloe groaned, then made puppy eyes at me. "At least tell me one thing: Did Drew and Taylor meet yet?"

"Nope. I've been with Drew the entire time until now. I haven't even seen Taylor, but Lexa signaled that things were okay with him a while ago. I hope he's still here."

Khloe and I turned away from the food, both of us scanning the room.

"It's too crazy in here," I said a few minutes later. "I don't see Jill or Cole, even."

"I'm sure Taylor wouldn't leave without saying good-bye," Khloe said. "But maybe he did want to go without interrupting you and Drew."

I turned back to the table and picked up my plate again. "I'm just glad that a serious fiasco was avoided and that Drew and Taylor each know the truth."

Khloe put a handful of cheese popcorn onto a plate. "And I know you—the party would have been ruined if

JEALOUSY

you felt guilty all night. Instead you're having fun, and so is everyone else."

I gave KK a one-armed hug. "Thanks to you, Lex, and Clare. You guys saved me during my Taylor thing."

Khloe gave me a sharp salute. "Sworn to best friend-ship duty, ma'am."

Giggling, we separated, and I finished getting snacks. I scanned the chairs for Drew and, thankfully, spotted him at a round table nearby.

"Who's the adorbs guy you came inside with?" Lacey asked, bouncing into step beside me. We had glee club and fashion class together.

"Um, that's Taylor," I said.

"More deets, Laur!" Lacey jerked her head toward the pool table. "Raquel and, well, all the girls are freaking out!"

I looked at the cluster of girls, who had gathered to watch a pool match.

I took a breath. I had to get used to explaining my rela-tionship to Taylor. No better time than now to get started.

"Taylor's a friend from home," I said. "He transferred to Canterwood."

Lacey's glossy coral mouth stretched into a wide grin. "Oh my God, he's going *here*?"

I nodded. "Now you've got the scoop. Talk later?"

I phrased it as a question, but it was more of a statement. We were strides away from Drew, and I didn't want to be discussing Taylor in front of him.

"Sure," Lacey said, flipping her long hair over one shoulder. "This is the *best* Halloween ever! A new hot guy on campus!" Lacey let out a little squeal and twirled on her heel, heading back in the direction of her friends.

I reached the table where Drew stood next to two chairs.

"Ooh, good choices," Drew said, eyeing the plate.

"I got to the snacks and desserts and felt like a little kid," I said. I slid into the chair that he pulled out for me.

He sat next to me. "How?"

I giggled. "There's *so* much candy and treats everywhere. I picked whatever I wanted, and it reminded me of Halloweens when my parents rationed candy to me and my sisters. Otherwise we'd eat our entire loot in one night and get sick."

Drew laughed and took a sip of one of the glass bottles of root beer he'd gotten for us. "I know exactly what you mean. After trick-or-treating one Halloween, my dad let me have some candy before he put it away. I was probably six or seven, I think."

"What was your costume?" I asked.

"Pirate," Drew answered.

We both laughed.

"Aw, did you have an eye patch and fake parrot?"

"I didn't say I was a lame pirate." He grinned. "My costume even had a plastic sword and stuff that made my teeth look black."

"Well, *excuse me*," I teased.

"After my dad went to bed, I found my candy. . . ."

"Uh-oh . . ." I covered my mouth, suppressing a laugh.

"Major. I ate *every* piece. Dad says he found me asleep on my bedroom floor the next morning with candy wrappers stuck to my face."

I laughed, taking a sip of my drink. "Did you get sick?"

"I'll just say that the next Halloween, I gladly gave my best friend all of my candy." Drew unwrapped a mini Snickers bar and took a bite. "But I think I got over it. Obviously."

We grinned at each other.

"Now I'm going to keep an eye on you, Adams. If the candy wrapper pile gets bigger than your head—I'm cutting you off."

Drew laughed. "I think that's fair."

His knee brushed mine, and the tingles where we'd touched made me wonder what it was going to feel like when we *kissed*.

I slid my gaze over, catching Drew looking at me.

"Tell me about a Lauren Towers Halloween," Drew said.

"Okay, hmmm . . ." I thought for a few seconds. "In third grade my teacher promised my class that if we all did well on our October vocabulary tests, we'd have a haunted house at our Halloween party at the end of the month."

"Good incentive to study," Drew said.

"For sure. We got to have the haunted house. I still remember the orange flyer that went home to our parents, asking for volunteers."

"Did your parents volunteer?" Drew asked. "I think third grade was the last year I was cool with my dad showing up at school events. Then it was 'I don't know you!' and I walked a million feet in front of him at all times."

Laughing, I twisted more in my seat to face him. "Third grade was the year for me too. I really wanted my parents to be at the party that year, but after that I went rogue."

Drew laughed.

"Mom couldn't because it was during a Friday afternoon and she had to work," I said. "Dad came."

"You said he's a writer and your mom's a lawyer, right?"

I loved that he remembered. "Right. I think he bought *Haunted Houses for Dummies* to help him. Dad and a bunch of other parents worked all day that Friday to set up a haunted house. My friends and I couldn't pay attention to anything—we kept 'stretching' and looking out the window. Parents were scurrying all over the recess field."

Drew smiled, flashing white teeth.

"What?" I asked, elbowing him. It was easy to be happy around him. He kept making me laugh.

"I like this story," he said. "You should be a writer."

I smiled. "No one's ever told me that before. Now the pressure's on to finish the story well." I sipped my drink. "*So*, our party was probably a couple of hours away when it started to *rain*. Actually, it wasn't just rain. It was a crazy, ridiculous downpour."

Drew hung his head. "Not cool."

"The downpour turned into a thunderstorm. Dripping-wet parents ended up in my classroom. My class freaked. My dad gathered the other parents, and I *knew* the party was going to be awesome. I just knew."

"Sounds like we both have pretty cool dads," Drew said.

I nodded. "Dad organized everything, and my class ended up with an amazing haunted house in the gym." I giggled. "Even the tough guys in my class screamed."

Squeeeeak!

Drew and I covered our ears. At the front of the room, the guilty culprit gave everyone a please-don't-kill-me smile. Khloe gave the wireless microphone in her hand an exasperated look.

"This mic is the best!" Khloe said, feigning seriousness. "That *squeak* feature totally got your attention. Now get on your feet!"

Everyone laughed.

As I stood, I swept my gaze over the room. There he was. Taylor stood near the front of the room. Four girls from my grade stood beside him. His attention was on Khloe, though, not Lacey and her friends.

No surprise that Tay's insta-popular, I thought. *He's fitting in, and it's only his first night.*

Lacey stepped back and whispered something to Raquel. Raquel nodded, pulled a compact mirror from her black sequin clutch, and passed it to Lacey. Lacey checked her reflection and carefully applied a sparkly pink lip gloss.

"The time has come," Khloe said, "to bring on the birthday toast!"

9

LUCKY NUMBER
THIRTEEN

"I'M KHLOE KINSELLA," SHE SAID WITH A smile. "Roommate of the birthday girl, Lauren Towers. Thank you all for coming, and I hope you've had a fun night. We have to start wrapping up the evening, since I promised we'd be out of the ballroom soon."

I glanced at the wall clock. *Whoa.* Tonight had gone by so fast.

"After the toast we'll cut the cake. Er, we'll have cupcakes."

I grinned at my roomie when her eyes landed on me.

"Happy birthday, Lauren," Khloe said. "It's your first birthday at Canterwood, and I hope it's one that you'll look back on and have good memories of. I'm beyond honored that you trusted me with planning your party. I'm so lucky that you're one of my closest friends *and* my roommate."

"Yay, Lauren!" someone cheered, and the room filled with applause.

Khloe clapped too, and minutes seemed to pass before everyone quieted down.

"Thirteen," Khloe said, "is a *big* deal, and I, along with all of your friends, hope your birthday wishes come true. I'm so happy you came to Canterwood and that we're besties. Mwah!" She touched her lips to her fingertips and blew me a giant kiss.

"There are a few more people who want to say happy birthday," Khloe added.

"Happy birthday!" Clare, Jill, and Lex sang into the mic. "We love you, LT!"

I flashed them the *I love you!* hand signal and couldn't stop smiling. I was the lucky one.

"Guests, please join us at the cupcake table to sing 'Happy Birthday' to Lauren," Khloe said. Her eyes settled on me. "And c'mon up here, LT."

"Come with me?" I whispered to Drew.

"Absolutely, birthday girl."

Drew held out his hand, and I slid mine into his.

The crowd parted, making a clear path for Drew and me. We walked across the ballroom and stopped near Khloe. The tiers of cupcakes looked *très* yummy! My parents had shipped cupcakes from Butter Lane, my favorite bakery in New York City. The huge strawberry cupcakes had vanilla icing that looked delicious.

One cupcake, slightly larger than the rest, was covered in confetti sprinkles and had a blue candle in the center.

Khloe picked up the cupcake, placed it on a round black plate, and held it out to Zack. He produced a Bic lighter and lit the candle wick.

"Happy birthday," he said, smiling at me.

"Thanks, Zack."

Khloe's guy was one of the first who had welcomed me to Canterwood. We'd been friends since day one.

"Guys?" Khloe asked, pursing her lips. "I think Laur needs to be a little, oh, *higher*."

"Wha—"

Before I could get the words out, Drew and Zack stood shoulder to shoulder. Garret and Cole put their hands gently on my waist, carefully lifting me into the air.

"Ah! Guys!" I squealed, giggling.

They lowered me onto Zack's and Drew's shoulders.

"You okay?" Drew asked, looking up at me.

"I feel like a princess!" I never, *ever* imagined something like this would happen during my birthday. I was literally swept off my feet and having one of the best nights of my life.

"Yay!" Khloe said. "Lex, your idea was *brill*."

"But are you all right?" I asked Drew. "Zack? Am I hurting you guys?"

Both guys shook their heads.

"Please, LT," Zack said. He used a deeper-than-normal voice. "Don't question our strength."

Nodding, I laughed. If Zack and Drew weren't careful, I'd be asking them to carry me everywhere.

Cole moved behind me, placing a steadying hand on my back. "We won't let you fall," he said. "Promise."

"Thanks, Cole," I said. His extra support did make me feel more stable. From my new seat, I could see over everyone's heads—the guys were taller than I'd thought.

Khloe stepped in front of me, lifting my cupcake and the flickering candle.

"It's like you're holding up an offering," I teased.

Khlo laughed. "Don't get too used to being up there, goddess."

Khloe led the room into singing "Happy Birthday."

They sang the *entire* song, and I was embarrassed when I started blinking back tears of happiness. I couldn't believe I was *here* at my dream school, surrounded by friends, and having the best birthday ever. Thirteen was *definitely* my lucky number.

IO

EX-BF, MEET MY
ALMOST-SORT-OF BF

"I'LL NEVER BE ABLE TO THANK YOU ENOUGH,"
I said, hugging Clare. People exited the ballroom as the party
ended. A bunch of people had pitched in to clean up and put
my gifts into bags, and Zack had left a note for the janitor
that we'd be back in the morning to clear out the decorations. It was late, and we had to get back to our rooms.

Clare tossed her red curls over her shoulder. "Omigod,
it was so much fun. I'm glad you had a good birthday!"

Next to me Lexa slung her arm across my shoulders.
"If you feel the need to repay us, you can, oh, tell us *everything* about Taylor tomorrow."

"Deal," I said. "I'm meeting up with him to talk, so I'll
BBM you guys after and we can hit The Sweet Shoppe."

I hugged Lex good night, and she and Clare headed

out. Zack had offered to walk Khloe back to Hawthorne a few moments ago. I'd waved the two of them off, promising Khlo that I'd be in our room in five.

With a happy sigh I turned around and walked toward the table with my PINK totes stuffed with Happy Birthday cards.

Drew and Taylor stood near my things. They weren't speaking to each other. Taylor's arms were crossed, and Drew's hands were in his pockets. Both of them stared in opposite directions.

Oh, mon Dieu!

I hurried over, my legs feeling heavy—like I was wearing ankle weights.

"Hi, hey," I babbled.

And I had nothing else.

What was I supposed to say to my almost-boyfriend and my ex?

"I wanted to say thanks for inviting me to your party," Taylor said. "I'm about to go back to Wren Hall."

I played with a sequin on my dress. "Thanks for coming. Um, Taylor, have you met Drew Adams?"

Taylor nodded, smiling.

Smiling?

"We met while you were saying good-bye to your

friends," Taylor said. He uncrossed his arms.

"Drew, I mentioned that Taylor's my friend from Union," I said. "We went to school together."

Drew, like Taylor, smiled. "That's what Taylor said."

The guys were being way cooler about this than I'd imagined. Maybe it wouldn't last a second after the clock struck midnight and it was officially not my birthday. But I'd take whatever civil behavior between them that I could get.

Taylor straightened, shifting his weight off the table. "I've got to go. 'Night, Lauren. Happy birthday."

We stared at each other for a millisecond before Taylor smiled, walked around me, and headed for the exit. Hugging Taylor in front of Drew didn't feel like it would have been right. Luckily, Taylor had made the decision about how to say good night for me.

The door closed behind Taylor, leaving Drew and me alone in the ballroom.

"Was that weird?" I asked. "Be honest."

"It was at first," Drew said. "I'm going to try not thinking about him as your ex."

I stared at the floor. I should have been there when they had met and . . .

"Laur?" Drew asked. "I see the look on your face. I was going to add that as much as I didn't want to like Taylor,

JEALOUSY

he might be okay. I mean, he had to be if you dated him. He's in your past. Everyone's got an ex. I'm not going to start any problems."

The sick feeling in my stomach started to disappear. "You're really okay after meeting Taylor? Really?"

"Really."

I threw my arms around Drew, almost knocking him over.

Laughing, he hugged me back.

"You're being so great about everything," I said. I let go of him, realizing that I'd just launched myself into his arms. "Thank you."

"No thanks necessary. Just let me ask two things?"

I met his eyes. They seemed to change shades with his mood.

"Can I walk you back to Hawthorne? And will you go out with me next week?"

I grinned. "Yes and yes!"

Drew picked up my bags, slinging them over one shoulder. I took his free hand and he enclosed it around mine. Together we walked across the silent ballroom and stepped out into the cool night air. Drew's hand in mine kept me warm the entire walk across campus to my dorm hall.

II

SIT AND SPILL!

THE SECOND I SHUT MY DOOR BEHIND ME, I ran across the room, grabbed my BlackBerry without even looking up, and started typing.

"Lauren, oh my God!" Khloe said. She was still in her party dress and had pulled her hair up into a cheer-leader-esque ponytail. "Sit and spill! Like, five minutes ago!"

I stopped typing, looking at her. "I will, promise. I'm BBMing Ana and Brielle first. I have to know *what* is going on."

Khloe nodded. "Totally understand. I'm going to change while you talk to them."

I nodded, looking back at the message I had already started to Ana. It was after ten, but Ana was a night owl, and her parents didn't mind if she texted or BBMed late once in a while.

Lauren:

Ana, r u up?

I sent the message. It delivered, and I waited for thirty seconds before writing again.

Y didn't u tell me abt Taylor??? All of a sudden, he was HERE and said u & Bri knew.

I hit send while the message before it was still unread.

He said he asked u guys not 2 tell me, but c'mon—girl code! Ana, it was srsly almost the biggest disaster!!! Taylor didn't just surprise me by coming, but he KISSED ME! U r obvi asleep, so I'll stop writing. We have 2 talk. Call me 2mrw?

Still standing, I exited out of Ana's name and clicked on Bri's.

Lauren:

Hey, r u there? I really need 2 talk 2 u . . .

I sent the message and waited. The *D* for delivered changed to an *R* for read!

Lauren:

OMG, so glad u r there!! Can u call me now? Or will parentals freak? If u can't at least we can BBM. I SO have 2 talk 2 u abt 2nite.

I kept my finger moving over the cursor to keep my

phone awake. I waited to see *Bri's writing a message* appear. But five minutes later nothing had changed. My second message was unread, and Bri hadn't written me back.

She's probably checking to see if her parents are asleep, I thought. *Then she's going to call you. That's why she's not writing back.*

Khloe came out of the bathroom, dress in hand, and had changed into a neon-yellow thermal long-sleeve shirt and pink flared pj pants.

"You getting any answers?" she asked.

I groaned. "No one's up. Well, Bri read my first BBM but not the second one. I think she's going to call, though."

"I'm sure. If she read your first message, then she's up. Maybe your phone has a bad signal?"

I checked the bars. I had full reception. "No, but I'll turn it off and on in case it's messed up."

Khloe opened the trunk at the foot of her bed and pulled out a plum-and-white-dotted throw blanket. She threw it across her bed and climbed under the covers.

I turned off my phone and kicked off my shoes. I sat at the edge of my bed and reopened BBM once my phone restarted.

Nothing.

Half an hour ticked by before I started my last message to Bri.

Lauren:

Going 2 sleep. Maybe talk 2 u 2mrw.

I punched the off button and put my phone facedown on my dresser. Khloe was reading the latest issue of *Celeb Dish* when I glanced over at her.

"I guess Bri couldn't call," I said. I tried to swallow the disappointment that I felt from Bri and Ana's secret keeping. "I'm going to get into pj's too."

In the bathroom I took off my dress and turned on the hot water in the sink. I splashed handfuls of it over my face and washed off my makeup. I pulled on black leggings and a warm button-down orange-and-black-striped shirt.

When I finally climbed into bed, I was so tired, I could barely keep my eyes open.

"I feel like I'm dreaming," I said to Khloe. "I had the best party imaginable, and this crazy thing happened in the middle of it."

"I'm so happy you had a good birthday," Khlo said. "Want to sleep now and save the boy talk for tomorrow morning? Over tea and pancakes?"

I covered a yawn. "Sounds good. Thank you, Khlo. For

everything. Tonight was the best party. You're the greatest best friend."

Khloe's voice was soft and soothing as she told me how much fun it had been to plan my party and how thrilled she was that I'd had fun. Her voice, making me feel comforted, helped me drift off to sleep before I'd even turned off my light.

12

SO LAST NIGHT
WAS REAL

IT WAS JUST AFTER TEN WHEN I ROLLED over and squinted at my clock. The shower was on, and I heard Khloe running lines for her lead role as Belle in *Beauty and the Beast*.

I sat up, a smile on my face as I thought about the fact that it was Saturday, Khloe would probably want to trail ride, and . . .

Flashes of last night flickered before my eyes like an old movie projector had appeared on our wall.

Masks.

Dresses.

Halloween decorations.

Laughter.

Music.

Taylor.

The Kiss.

Fighting.

Drew.

Dancing.

Cupcakes.

Ana.

Brielle.

I shook my head, trying to stop the visions.

Taylor was here. On campus. It hadn't been a dream. He had really been at my party last night, and I *really* had to get some answers today. Brielle and Ana owed me.

I picked up my phone and turned it on. There were two voice mails and two BBMs.

I checked BBM first.

Ana:

I can't even begin to say how sorry I am. Telling u that over BBM is lame. Check ur voice mail. xx A

Becca:

Little sister! (OK, *teenage sister*) How was last nite? Did Khloe throw u an amaze party? She better have or I'll have 2 talk 2 her @ Parents' Weekend. Call me!!

I pressed the button for voice mail and put my phone

on speaker. The automated voice announced the first new message.

"Lauren, hi. It's Ana. It's about nine a.m. and I just got your BBMs from last night." There was a long pause. "Okay, I didn't just get them. I read them about an hour ago and waited this long to call. I was scared because I know how mad you must be. I'm not blaming you at all—I deserve it. I think . . . I think you really need to talk to Taylor and Brielle. The phone's going to cut me off, but I'm here if you want to call, IM, BBM, Skype—anything. I love—"

"Next new message," cut in the robotic voice.

"Heeey! LT!" Brielle's bubbly voice filled the room. She talked faster than Ana, so she'd probably be able to fit more into her message. Hopefully, an explanation. "OMG, I'm SO sorry about last night! I read your message, went to check on my parents, and started to dial you. My Dad's freaky batlike hearing must have heard me dial or something! He came into my room and saw me with my phone." Brielle sighed. "He went through the whole 'you can't talk on the phone after ten' blah-blah-blah speech, and he took my BlackBerry. I tried to tell him that it was you and very important. I mean, hello, it was your birthday, but nope. Anyway, let's totes talk! I'm home all day. Love you, bestie!"

I hung up, plugging in my almost-dead phone to charge. The bathroom door opened, releasing a cloud of steam and pumpkin-spice-scented body wash—one of the fall beauty products Khloe and I had bought and shared.

"Hey," Khloe said. She wore her thick hot-pink terry-cloth robe and matching slippers. Her long blond hair was up, turban-style, in a teal towel.

"You been up long?" I asked. I walked over and picked up the bag of birthday cards that I hadn't had a chance to open last night.

"I just got up and hopped in the shower. I didn't wake you, did I?"

"Not at all. How was shower rehearsal?" I grinned at her.

Khloe opened her dresser drawer and pulled out clothes. "It was perfect, thank you very much. I know all of my lines, and I get more and more excited every day. I can't wait for opening night."

"Me either. You're going to do great."

Khloe smiled her thanks and changed into jeans and a gray cable-knit sweater and started detangling her hair.

"I had messages on my phone," I said. "Brielle and Ana."

Khloe sat on her desk chair, swiveling it toward me. "Everything okay?"

I nodded. "It was exactly what I thought last night. Bri got caught with her phone, and her dad took it. Ana called and left a super-apologetic message and said she wanted to talk. I really can't be too mad at them for this. They're my best friends—I know they must have thought that Taylor coming to my party was the ultimate surprise. I can't blame them for what Taylor decided to do when he got here."

Khloe rubbed a few drops of Ojon Serum on her hands and massaged it into her hair. "You're right about that. I bet things will clear up even more once you talk to them."

"I'm sure. I'll get in touch with them later. Right now I just want a break from the whole thing."

Bing!

I picked up my phone and saw a new BBM.

Taylor:

Hey, Laur. U still want 2 talk 2day? I'm free whenever.

"Okay, the break will have to wait a while. Taylor," I explained. "He still wants to meet today. I was thinking about asking him to meet me at the stable. He could see Whisper, and after we talk, I wondered if you'd be into a trail ride."

"That's only the best weekend idea ever," Khlo said. "You want me to see if Cole and anyone else wants to come? Or are you in the mood for KK and LT time?"

I smiled. "The second option, if that's cool with you."

"Definitely."

"I'm going to text Taylor and see if he wants to meet in half an hour. I'll message you after?"

"That's perf," Khloe said.

I pulled back my covers. "Ohhh, wait. I forgot—we have to clean up the ballroom. There are still decorations on the walls and tables and chairs to put away."

Khloe shook her head. "Did you really think I'd let you clean up after your own party? Puh-lease."

"Who did?"

"The guys. Zack, Garret, a bunch of their friends, Drew, and Cole were on cleanup duty. They already texted me that the ballroom is back in pre-party shape."

"Aw, that was sweet of them. You really thought of everything, Khlo."

Khloe grinned, then stuck out her tongue. "Stop seeming so surprised." She started clipping her hair into sections to blow-dry, and I picked up my phone. I opened BBM.

Lauren:

U up 4 mtg @ the stable? I'm going trail riding w Khloe after u and I talk.

Taylor is writing a message appeared seconds later.

Taylor:

Sounds good. I'm excited 2 c Whisper. ☺ When?

Lauren:

30 mins? Do u know how 2 get there?

Taylor:

Yeah, I actually passed it when I arrived.

Lauren:

OK. BBM me if u get lost or something. Wisp's stall is near end of aisle on left. C u in a bit! ☺

I exited out of my convo with Taylor and clicked on Becca's name.

Lauren:

Khloe threw the BEST party ever!! Srsly, wait till u c the pix when I upload them 2 FaceSpace. I had an amazing bday . . . and a VERY unexpected surprise. Will fill u in ltr—promise! Love u & miss u! xoxo

While Khloe dried her hair, I grabbed a single-serving bottle of OJ from our mini-fridge and a raspberry breakfast bar. While I ate, I opened some of my birthday cards. The number of cards was overwhelming. Everyone had done exactly what I had wished for. The cards either held cash for me to donate to my fave horse charity or had a printed screen shot of their donation.

I pulled a card in a sparkly light-blue envelope from the pile. Immediately I recognized the handwriting.

Taylor's.

I opened the envelope, and inside was a printed receipt for his donation. *One hundred dollars.*

"Oh my God," I whispered to myself. Taylor's family was comfortable enough to make such a donation, but I knew Taylor hadn't asked them for the money. He'd spent his allowance—a *big* part of it—on me.

The card was gorgeous—black with light-blue swirls and a scripty "Happy Birthday!" font.

I read his message.

Lauren,

Happy Birthday! I can't believe you're older than ME! Not fair! ☺ I'll catch up with you soon, though. If you're reading this card and things worked out the way I hoped they would, then I'm a student at Canterwood too. I'll always be only minutes away if you need anything. You deserve to have a killer thirteenth birthday, and I hope all of your wishes come true.

~T

I smiled, tucking the card back into the envelope. I couldn't wait to gather all of the checks and send them to the retired-racehorse charity. I rifled through the pile, picking out cards from Becca, my parents, Ana, and Brielle. But I'd have to read them later. It was time to meet Taylor.

13

NOT INTERESTED

THE FIRST DAY OF NOVEMBER WAS COMFORT-ably cool. I zipped my coffee-colored wool jacket. The frisky horses definitely felt the drop in temperature. A herd of seven or eight horses played, nipping each other's necks and darting up the hill at a full gallop.

In the big arena, Mr. Conner was trotting a gray gelding in a large circle. The young horse had arrived a few days ago and was one of the horses that Mr. Conner was train-ing. I knew the gelding's name was Lexington and that he had been brought to Mr. Conner with only basic training. Lexa said she'd heard that the owner was trying to make the United States Equestrian Team and was too busy training his other, more seasoned horses to work with Lexington. It was Mr. Conner's job to train the young horse and feel out his potential. I crossed my fingers that I'd see Lexington competing at the Rolex Kentucky years from now when he was much older and competing in the top show circuit.

I stopped, stepping off the sidewalk and onto the grass to watch Mr. Conner ride. Lexington showed how green he was from his uneven trot to his jerky transition to a canter, but he seemed willing to work. It seemed as though the pair had been at work for a while—Lexington's coat was steely gray around his saddle pad, and bits of froth from his mouth working the bit flecked against his chest.

Mr. Conner was a quiet rider—exactly what Lexington needed. The stillness of Mr. Conner's hands and legs seemed to work with keeping Lexington calm. I watched them for minutes, even though I could have stood there all day. My eyes didn't know where to look as I tried to follow Mr. Conner's aids to Lexington. Mr. Conner was the kind of rider that I hoped to be someday.

Reluctantly I left the pair to practice in private and walked into the stable. I walked down the aisle, oddly quiet for a late Saturday morning, and noted that most of the horses wore light blankets. Almost every horse had their finely sculpted head stuck over their stall door. Necks craned in my direction, and there was an occasional whinny or neigh as the horses talked back and forth.

Near the end of the aisle, I spotted a bay and a gray with their heads together. It was as if they were using ESP to have a secret conversation.

"Don't let me interrupt," I said, smiling at them.

Ever, Khloe's bay horse, swiveled her head toward me. In the stall next to her, Whisper, my gray mare, pricked her ears and let out a soft grunt.

"Hi, pretties," I said. I didn't want Ever to feel left out, so I stood between the two horses and scratched their cheeks.

"I'm sure Khloe is going to come see you very soon, Ever-girl," I told Khloe's mare. "Take a nap—it's the weekend!" I gave the mare a final pat and moved to Whisper's stall. Her brass nameplate with her name etched into it had a fingerprint smudge on it. I used my sleeve to wipe it clean before unlatching the stall door.

"Hi, hi, hi," I said to Whisper. I put my arms around her neck, hugging her. "You smell so good! I'm so happy to see you."

Whisper's winter coat was starting to grow in. Her sleek gray body was filling out with fuzzy longer hair to keep her warm.

I looked her over—from big brown eyes and long eyelashes to adorable pink-and-black snip. Each time I saw Whisper, it was almost as if I was seeing her for the first time. It was still hard to believe that she was mine. My parents had surprised me with the gift of my first horse when I'd been accepted to Canterwood. I'd met several horses before seeing Whisper. It had been love at first sight.

I stood on tiptoes to reach Whisper's ear. "We're going trail riding with Khloe and Ever," I said, keeping my voice low. "But first Taylor's coming. Here. To talk."

Whisper leaned her head into me, pushing her muzzle against my collarbone. "Ohhh," I said, laughing. "You're as bad as Khloe! You want details. Well, *mon amour*, you'll have to wait until we hit the trails."

I rubbed my hand down Whisper's forehead, over her muzzle, and under her chin. I looked down the aisle. A few students had horses in crossties, and the hot walker had four horses walking in cooling circles. A familiar hat— UConn Huskies—popped into view, and Taylor and I saw each other at the same time.

I waved and he smiled, heading toward me. I'd given him the University of Connecticut hat after we'd been dating a while.

"What do you think?" I asked. "Is this stable insane or what?"

Taylor's eyes roamed from the stalls, to the loft, to the empty wash stall. "It's gorgeous, Laur. Wow. This type of

space to practice in and keep Whisper must be so condu-
cive to good lessons."

"Absolutely. But I don't want to take away anything
from Briar Creek. I learned so much about who I am and
what I want while I was there. I'd never be *here* if it weren't
for Briar Creek and Kim."

Taylor shook his head. "I don't think you're knocking
BC at all. They are both different places with their own
strengths that help you and Whisper in different ways."

Whisper, hearing her name, stretched her neck and
bumped Taylor's arm with her muzzle.

"Hey!" Taylor laughed. "I'm sorry, Princess Whisper. I
was just about to say hi to you."

Taylor had spent lots of afternoons at Briar Creek
with me over the summer, and I loved how comfy he and
Whisper were with each other.

Taylor scratched under Whisper's forelock, one of her
favorite spots, and she closed her eyes in bliss.

"She's glad to see you," I said. "Clearly, I never pet her
or pay any attention to her at all."

Taylor nodded. "I can tell. Whisper's starved for attention. I don't know how you couldn't pet this pretty girl
all of the time."

We both started laughing, and Whisper eyed the two

of us. I started telling Taylor about the stable and how different it was from Briar Creek. When Taylor stopped scratching her, Wisp moved her head to near me. When I got caught up in our conversation and didn't give Whisper affection, she turned back to Taylor.

"Look at yourself," I said to Whisper, my tone teasing. "You're not interested in hanging out with us at all unless you're getting petted or scratched. Jeez, Wisp."

The mare shook her head and neck, sending her mane flying.

"I was thinking that we could go for a walk," I said. "I could show you around campus, and we'd be able to talk privately. That okay?"

"That's perfect," Taylor said. "I haven't seen the pool or gym yet, so I'm excited about those."

"I go to the pool all the time to—" I stopped midsentence. I'd been about to say that I frequented the pool to watch Drew swim and cheer him on during practice. "To study. It's, um, surprisingly calming with, you know, the water."

With my face hiding behind Whisper's head, I rolled my eyes at my flub.

"Cool, let's go," Taylor said.

14

LT, TOUR GUIDE

I LED TAY OUT OF THE STABLE, AND WE walked side by side up the sidewalk. I veered left and took one of the less populated routes.

"You probably know that building," I said, pointing to one. "Administration."

"I have to go there tomorrow morning," Taylor said. "I've got an appointment with the guidance counselor—"

"Ms. Utz," we finished together.

"She's Canterwood royalty," I said. "Once you meet her, you'll never forget Ms. Utz."

"Explain, please."

I stepped on a crunchy brown leaf with my paddock boot. "Can't, sorry. She's actually quite . . . *indescribable*."

We walked past a few more buildings, and I motioned

toward them and told Taylor any extra facts. A slight breeze made leaves tumble across the raked lawn, and I inhaled a big gulp of fresh fall air.

"How was last night?" I asked. "The party. People. Your roommate."

Taylor stuck his hands into the kangaroo pocket of his black fleece pullover. He was casual, but pulled together, in the pullover, dark-wash jeans, his broken-in blue-and-white University of Connecticut hat, and Converse sneakers.

"Your birthday was really fun," Taylor said. "Your friends know how to throw a serious party! Especially Khloe. She was hilarious, and her toast was awesome. I want her and the rest of your friends to plan my next birthday."

"Somewhere on this giant campus," I said, "Khloe Kinsella's feeling like she's having a sugar rush. She'll be able to sense that someone's saying good things about her."

"Well, it seems like you and I both lucked out, big-time, in the roommate department," Taylor said. "My roommate, Matthew, is cool. He was in our room when I got back, and we got along right away. He asked me to play a new game on his Xbox, and we played for hours."

"That was nice of him."

Taylor stretched his arms to the sky. "It was a no-pressure way to get to know each other. I almost freaked out for a minute, because I kind of forgot where I was. Like, I expected my dad to come in, see me 'wasting my time' playing a video game, and get mad at me."

"Tay," I said, touching his arm. "I'm sorry."

"I'm not. I'm *here.* Matt and I played as long as we wanted, and no one made me feel bad for doing something that wasn't schoolwork or somehow related to learning about finances or business."

Quiet anger seeped through me. Mr. Frost had really come down on Taylor even more since I'd been gone.

I motioned for Taylor to follow me onto another side-walk that forked away from the main one. "That's great! What about this morning? Did your stuff come?"

"Movers were here at nine, and they unloaded my stuff like they were trying to break a record. Matt even got up and helped me move boxes from the hallway into our room. That saved me a ton of time."

"I really can't wait to meet this guy," I said. "You're *très* right—we both got amazing roomies."

"I liked Khloe, Lexa, and the rest of your friends that I met last night too," Taylor said. He hopped over a crack in the sidewalk. "I hope you didn't think that I was staying away from you on purpose. I mean, I guess I kind of was, because I wanted to give you and Drew space." He grinned. "Did you tell Lacey to talk to me all night?"

I frowned. "What? No. Why do you ask?"

"She came up to me, introduced herself and her friends," Taylor said. He readjusted his hat. "The way Lacey talked to me—like, asking me a zillion questions about myself, offering to show me around school, stuff like that—I thought you or somebody asked her to make sure I had someone to talk to at the party."

A weird feeling of *jealousy* burned in my chest. There was no reason for me to be jealous! I'd been the one who had told Taylor that I didn't want to get back together. Drew made me beyond happy, and I wanted nothing more than to keep hanging out with him and exploring a possible relationship.

"That's Lacey's personality," I said. "I'm glad she kept you company last night. She didn't drive you crazy, did she?"

"No way," Taylor said. "She's a cool girl, and I like getting to know your friends."

I opened my mouth to tell him that Lacey and I weren't friend-friends like Khloe, Lexa, Clare, Jill, and I were, but

I stopped myself. Taylor had to get to know people on campus.

As if we'd timed our walk perfectly, the gym was just ahead.

"Those tennis courts close in a couple of weeks," I said, pointing to the empty courts. "And the outdoor pool's already closed."

We passed by the Olympic-size pool, which had been drained and covered until next year. Taylor craned his neck to inspect every inch of it, and the giant smile on his face reinforced my guess that he was impressed.

I took Taylor to the side of the gym that housed the indoor pool. I pulled open the frosted glass door, and he followed me inside. No one was in the pool or the stands, so it was just Taylor and me.

His green eyes widened as he took in the pool. Canterwood's pool was bigger than Yates's, and it had more rows of bleachers for people to watch from. There was even a diving board at the pool's deep end.

"What do you think?" I asked. "Is it up to Taylor Frost's swimming standards?"

"Um, *yeah*!" Taylor walked over to the pool, crouched down, and touched the water with his left fingers. "I saw the pictures online, but man, they need a new photographer.

This pool is killer. I can't wait to start practicing and get on the team."

"I know you'll make the team." I paused. "Drew's on it."

Taylor stood, keeping his eyes on the pool. "Oh. Cool. Then I'll know someone if I make it."

"Want to sit in here since it's empty and talk for a few?" I asked.

Taylor nodded, and we climbed onto the highest row of bleachers and rested our backs against the wall.

I shifted on the bench. I had questions, but I didn't know if I was ready to hear the answers to some of them.

"It was hard for me starting at Canterwood at the beginning of the school year," I said. "I can't imagine how much pressure you feel about starting mid-semester." I took a breath. "Taylor, I know everything about your dad and why you wanted to transfer. But were you *really* that afraid of being taken off the swim team that you decided to change schools now?"

Taylor took several seconds before looking at me. "Yes, I was. But I'm not going to lie. Like I told you last night, there were other factors. Like my dad's nonstop business talk. And . . . you."

"You didn't come here *just* for me, though, right?"

"No. I knew there was a chance you had already met

somebody, but I had to try. You attending the school that just happened to be perfect for me was a bonus. A big one."

I smiled. "Thanks."

"I wanted—and still want—us to be together. But for now I'm going to have to be okay at just being friends. I don't really know *how* to be okay with that, but I'll figure it out." He stopped, a faraway look in his eyes before they focused again. "You and I hung out all summer and were cool with each other. I missed that. There's been a huge hole in my life since you've been gone. I really missed your friendship—not just having you as my girlfriend."

"I missed you, too. I may have met some wonderful and amazing friends, but I have moments every day when I want to see Bri or Ana or you and tell you something exciting or vent about something that's bugging me."

Taylor nodded. We stayed in the gym, talking about what we'd missed in each other's lives since I'd gone to Canterwood. I shared my schedule and told Taylor which teachers to avoid if possible.

"Thanks, Laur," Taylor said nearly an hour later. "I'm glad we got the chance to catch up."

"Me too." I leaned over and gave him a quick, one-armed hug. "What are you doing the rest of the weekend?"

"Unpacking," Taylor said. "Then I've got a checklist of stuff I'm supposed to do that was in my welcome packet."

We stood and made our way down the bleachers.

"If you start to get overwhelmed, text me," I said. "This place can be a little scary at first. But I'm sure you've got it."

I reached to open the door to go outside. Before I grasped the handle, the door swung in the opposite direction, and chilly air swept inside the humid pool area.

"Hi!" Raquel said. She was in flip-flops and a pink Puma tracksuit. A matching duffel bag was over one shoulder.

"Hey," Taylor and I said.

Raquel's long black hair was in a French braid, and she shot a smile at us both, but *really* looking at Taylor.

"What're you guys doing?" Raquel asked. "I hope I didn't interrupt anything. . . ." She put down her bag on one of the lowest bleacher rungs and pulled out a green Canterwood Crest towel with the school's name stitched in gold.

"You didn't. I was giving Taylor a tour of campus," I said. "He's a swimmer, so—"

"Omigod!" Raquel cut in. "You swim? Me too!" She unzipped her Puma jacket, revealing a yellow bathing suit.

The light color made her darker skin stand out. "I'm on the girls' swim team."

"That's awesome," Taylor said, smiling. "I'll definitely be trying out for the guys' team."

"We should totally practice together sometime," Raquel said. She kicked off her flip-flops, and I noted the metallic lilac polish on her toes matched her fingernails. Raquel definitely looked pool perfect. She flashed Taylor a giant smile, her teeth white against her naturally berry-colored lips.

"That would be fun," Taylor said. "I'll see you around."

Raquel gave him another grin. "See ya."

This time Taylor held the door open for me, and the smell of chlorine disappeared when we walked a few steps away from the building.

"I think you're going to be just fine at Canterwood," I said. "You've already got Lacey *and* Raquel almost begging you to ask them out. I bet Raquel looks up your e-mail in the student directory and there's already a message in your in-box inviting you to swim with her."

Taylor turned to me, his eyes meeting mine. "Lacey and Raquel are nice, but neither of them are the girl that I'm interested in."

15

LOVE TRIANGLE

"HE SAID *WHAT*?"

"Khloe!" I said. "We might be in the woods, but I think everyone on campus heard that. And you may have just deafened a bunch of squirrels!"

Khloe hunched a little in Ever's saddle, making an *oops* face. "Sorry. You know that I get crazy-excited about this stuff. I cannot believe that Taylor said no to Lacey and Raquel *to your face* after you told him the night before that you were with Drew."

"I know!" My own comment came out louder than necessary too. We both giggled. "Please tell me this whole Taylor-slash-Drew thing isn't going to be awkward forever," I moaned.

Khloe reached over and patted my knee with her

leather-gloved hand. "Aw, LT. We'll figure it out. Taylor just got here. I'm sure once he really sees that you and Drew are on your way to superstar coupledom, then he'll back off."

Beneath me Whisper snorted as if she agreed with Khloe. Once I'd said good-bye to Taylor, I'd BBMed Khloe and asked if she was ready to ride. We'd rushed to tack up our horses and get on our favorite trail as fast as possible so we could talk without anyone overhearing.

"I mean," Khloe said, tapping a finger against her chin, "did you guys even talk about *Taylor's* dating life since you've been gone?"

I shook my head. "He would have told me if he'd dated anyone. Plus, the way he's talked about wanting to get back together makes me think he hasn't been on a date since our breakup."

"You're probably right," Khloe said. "Ah, this whole thing! Two guys. Both total opposites of the other. Black hair. Blond hair. Tan. Pale. Rider. Swimmer." She frowned. "Oh, I forgot that Drew and Taylor both swim. Two boys pining after one *very* lucky girl."

"Am I? Are you sure?"

"Hello, nothing's more fun than a Canterwood love triangle!"

16

DOES SOMEONE HAVE
A SECRET?

Lauren Towers's Blog

9:02 p.m.: ??? **super**-locked post for approved friends only*

Permission granted for this post: Lexa Reed, Clare Bryant, Becca Towers, and Khloe Kinsella. (Because it's so secure, I'm going to write out full names, unlike before, when I used initials.)

Okay, so . . . today was, like, Taylor 24/7. After I met with him, I rode with Khloe and filled her in from beginning to end about my party and my earlier talk with Taylor. She was *shocked*, to put it mildly. What's really crazy—and what we can't figure out—is the Bri and Ana thing.

After riding, Khlo and I took showers, and when I got out, she said someone had called. It was Ana. Again. That's not unusual, because when I lived at home, we'd call each other a million times a day. Sometimes I'd even call just to leave an EBT on their voice mails!

But before Ana called, I'd BBMed her when Khloe and I got back to our room, saying I'd call her later tonight.

While Khloe was showering, I opened my cards from Bri and Ana.

After opening Ana's card, I couldn't stand to call her later. Her card was call-her-right-now-worthy!

I dialed her and got voice mail. I thanked her for calling about the Taylor Thing and said I wanted to definitely talk more. But I ended it on a *très* lighter note by promising to buy her a grande peppermint mocha from Starbucks every day this holiday break. Why? Because she actually *fund-raised* at Yates for my retired-racehorse charity!

Ana, living up to her AnaArtiste Chatter handle, had hand-painted my card. She'd covered it in a rainbow of colors that made swirls, hearts, and stars. I'm looking at it now, and it's absolutely *magnifique*!

When I opened the card, a check fell out along with photos. When I bent down to pick it up, I fell back onto the carpet. Ana had obviously worked insanely hard, judging from the amount of the check.

I read the note inside the card. Ana's writing made me teary.

LaurBell,

Haaappy birthday! I hope you know how much
I love you and miss you. Nothing's the same
without you. I still look for you in every class and
am still shocked when you're not there. I hope
the check helps the retired-racehorse charity. Bri
and I took some pics and had Kim take a couple
of us with Zane and Breeze. Hopefully, they'll
make you smile!

Counting down the days until break!! ☺

xoxo,

~Ana

I flipped through the photos—hungry-like—for anything that showed me home. In one pic Ana is smiling down
from Breeze's back. The strawberry roan mare's ears were
pointed forward at the camera, and the sky was a brilliant
blue above them. They were in front of one of the small
paddocks at Briar Creek.

Another pic was of Bri washing Zane. He is my old

instructor Kim's horse, but Bri is the only one who rides him. Bri's tongue was stuck out at the camera, and she had a giant purple sponge covered in bubbles. Zane needs constant baths—the albino shows every speck of dirt.

There were a few photos from school. Friends waving or flashing the peace sign at the camera.

There was a great one of Ana with her guy Jeremy's arm wrapped around her. Bri was on Ana's other side, and Taylor's arm was slung across her shoulders. All four of them grinned into the camera. Looking at that photo made me miss Yates a little. My teachers. My friends. But I pinned the photo to my corkboard, ultimately happy to have a picture of my friends together. Now Taylor is here, and that's one friend at Canterwood from home.

My favorite picture, though, was of Ana and Brielle. They probably had Kim take it, because they were in the driveway of Briar Creek. The sun was just starting to set, and they were each on their horse, bareback. It looked like they'd just come to the stable to play—both of them sported jean cutoffs. Zane wore a blue halter and Breeze had a purple halter, and Ana and Brielle had knotted their lead lines to one side of the halter to act as reins. The purple-pink-orange-streaked sky behind them looked like one of Ana's paintings.

There was a card from Bri, too, which was my taste—sky blue with tiny silver and gold stars made from shiny foil. Confetti stars, just like the ones on the card, flew everywhere when I opened it—not expecting the surprise. The stars fell around a check—Bri had given me all of her allowance and convinced her parents to match her donation. Inside she'd written the sweetest message:

Laur,

Omigod, BFFL! You're *13* today! I wish I could be there to party with you (and, you know, show off my fab dancing skills), but you *do* have one Union friend there. I feel so lucky to celebrate another year as your best friend. It doesn't matter if you're 5,000 miles away—we'll always be as tight as if you were home. Now stop reading, go do something fun, and pretend this card is a giant hug from your girl—Brielle! ☺

♥ ♥,

B

I called Bri, too, dying to thank her. Like my phone call to Ana, Brielle's phone rang until it went to voice mail. I left a quick message and asked her to call me.

After I read those cards, it made things even more confusing about Ana and Brielle. I showed Khloe the cards and checks. Khloe did a dramatic performance of what she envisioned happening when I handed over the checks to charity.

"It'll be like you combined all of the money," Khloe said, unable to sit still. "You'll have a giant cardboard check covered with a red cloth that you're about to unveil. Even the Thoroughbreds will be watching!"

I loved her story, even though that was definitely *not* going to happen. Especially since I didn't know how to get a giant cardboard check.

Ack! I've rambled forever! Sorry! Almost done— promise! One of the most important things I wanted to write about was Bri and Ana. It feels like we've been drifting apart since I've been here. The old Ana and the Brielle I knew would have told me about Taylor. Or, on the extremely crazy-slash-ridiculous chance they didn't, Ana and Bri would have flooded me with BBMs, texts, calls, *fireworks* to get my attention to explain after Taylor got here.

If I know my friends, they are probably both feeling

guilty, and that could explain the short, zero-details messages. I'd played Ana's message for Khloe, and that was the one, though, that we were stuck on. Why did Ana suggest I talk to Bri? Is Bri keeping a secret?

Posted by Lauren Towers

17
MAYBE WE SHOULD MICROCHIP TAYLOR

"DO YOU THINK WE'RE GOING TO SEE HIM?" I asked Khloe. My roomie and I stood in the hallway of Hawthorne early Monday morning.

Khloe locked our dorm room door and tossed the keys into her bag. "Probably. But remember, I promised to step in and try to help Taylor if I can, if he's lost or whatever. That will keep things at minimum weirdness between you and Drew. And right now minimum weirdness would be the maximum awesomeness."

"Did I mention that I have the best roommate?" I slung an arm across her shoulders as we started to the Hawthorne exit door. "I'm *so* nervous. Ridiculously nervous. I know that Drew's not going to be like, 'I saw you talking to Taylor outside the science building.

See ya.' But this whole thing is just weird!"

Khloe nodded, flipping her fishtail braid over her shoulder. She'd teased her hair near the crown and had slipped on the skinniest of black headbands. I'd convinced her to secure the braid with a black leather tie. The look was *très* chic.

"It's going to be strange for a while. It just *is*," Khloe said. She stopped short of opening the door. "Main goal is that you try to stay focused on two things: One is that you and Drew are together, and keeping your relationship moving forward is most important. And two, you and Taylor are friends. *Juuust* friends. It doesn't mean you can't talk to him and hang out, but just think about how you'd feel if Drew suddenly started hanging with one of his exes-turned-friends."

I wiped sweaty palms on the black pants I'd paired with black-and-white oxfords. The shoes were my new obsession. I'd added an ivory cashmere-blend sweater to complete the look.

"You're right. Definitely will keep that in mind." I took a deep breath.

"Ready?" Khloe put her hand on the door handle.

"Let's go."

I shivered when we stepped outside. The November air

stung my face and hands. Khloe and I huddled together against the cold.

"At least Mr. Davidson's class isn't too far away," she said through chattering teeth.

"Or maybe we should have checked the weather this morning and worn coats like everyone else."

I tipped my chin ahead of us at the rainbowlike coats that dotted campus. Puffy coats. Wool peacoats. Long coats. Vests. It really looked as though everyone *but* us had checked their weather app this morning.

As we neared the English building, I had a sense of *Yes! Made it without seeing Tay.* It wasn't that I *didn't* want to see Taylor, but I also wanted to be considerate of Drew's feelings.

I walked into Mr. Davidson's class and took my usual seat. I opened my notebook, going to my pages of notes. My academic planner had *Study for Caged Bird midterm!* written on every other day's space.

Khloe sat at the desk next to me and waved at Clare when she walked into the room.

"Hey, hey," Clare said. Her red hair was in a half updo, and long curls cascaded down her back.

"Love the sweater," I said. "That shade of green is great with your hair."

Clare beamed. "Thank you! I got this on sale from Kohl's."

Her hunter-green sweater was supercute—LOVE was scrawled across the chest in a scripty, gold font.

Clare sat next to Khloe—the desks were arranged in a large circle—and started unloading her book bag. I went back to my calendar, and there was so much coming up—Parents' Weekend, Thanksgiving break, midterms, Christmas break—

"Lauren!"

I looked up at the voice that had chirped at me.

Lacey slid into the desk next to me. She dropped her pink bag and wildly pushed her light-brown bangs out of her eyes. Her hair was pulled into the highest ponytail I'd ever seen—one that I couldn't imagine *not* getting a headache from.

"Hi," I said. "How ar—"

"Is he in this class? What's his schedule? We've all been trying to guess, and I looked for him everywhere this morning." Lacey was almost breathless when she'd finished.

"You mean Taylor?" I asked, already knowing the answer.

"Um, yeah! Laur, you're the one with all the info. You're his ex. Even better—you're still his *friend*."

I bristled a little at the way Lacey said "friend." Taylor wasn't my boyfriend, but I wasn't exactly ready to give Lacey the 411 on all things Taylor Frost.

"He's not in this class," I said. "And I actually don't know his full schedule."

"You aren't talking to him?" Lacey asked. She raised an eyebrow like she didn't believe me.

"No—I mean *yes,* I am, but Taylor's settling into campus and I'm busy with classes, riding, and stuff."

Lacey sat back in her seat a little. "Oh. Gotcha. I'll find out on my own." Her tone was clipped.

Before I could even respond, she turned to one of her friends who had just sat next to her. Lacey whispered something and shot me an annoyed look over her shoulder.

Not wanting to be like Lacey, I took out my phone and typed a BBM.

Lauren:

Did u c what Lacey just did?

Khloe:

No! What?

Lauren:

She was asking me abt Taylor and

I shoved my phone under my desk and put my gaze on the front of the classroom as Mr. Davidson entered.

"Good morning, everyone," he greeted us.

"Good morning, Mr. Davidson," we all said back.

The rest of the forty-five-minute period wasn't good. At least not for me. Lacey only looked at me once during class, and when she did, her eyes were narrowed and her lips were pressed together. Her attitude had spread via whispers and under-the-desk texting to almost every other girl in class.

One by one I got a stare and then a look of disgust from my classmates. I'd never counted down the seconds until a class's end the way I did in today's English period.

Thirty seconds left.

I tore my eyes away from the second hand on the clock and did something I knew Mr. Davidson hated—I started packing before he finished talking.

Clare and Khloe had BBMed me during the entire class, telling me not to let Lacey and her friends make me feel bad. We'd been on our phones so much, I couldn't believe we hadn't gotten caught.

I closed my notebook. The lined page was blank except for a date and *Notes*. I doubted that Khloe and Clare had taken notes either.

". . . and that sums up today's discussion," Mr. Davidson

said as I tuned back in. The blond teacher stood, smiling at us. "We'll pick up with the final chapter of *I Know Why the Caged Bird Sings* on Wednesday. Heads up—there will be a quiz tomorrow on today's discussion."

Mr. Davidson let his gaze linger on me. Then Khloe. Then Clare. Then Lacey.

"If you didn't take notes," he said, "I hope you'll be able to borrow a friend's. See you all tomorrow."

Oh, mon Dieu. The way Mr. Davidson had looked at me made me wish I could evaporate. He *knew* I hadn't been paying attention, and he was disappointed. Letting down a teacher made me feel awful.

I gathered my book and notebook into my arms, not even bothering to put them into my backpack. In a daze I bolted for the door, barely avoiding a collision with a classmate. I was *not* going to let a mean girl make me cry. But even as I repeated that over and over to myself, tears blurred my vision as I waited for Clare and Khloe outside the classroom.

18

THIS FEELS LIKE
A BAD MOVIE

BY LUNCH I FELT LIKE I WAS A CHARACTER IN a teen movie. I was the Liked Ten Seconds Ago Girl who had done or said something that caused all of my Used to Like Me Friends to become the Whispering Mean Girls.

I didn't look up from my spot at the corner table in the back (*very* back) of the caf, which Khloe and Clare had chosen. Lexa had joined us, and while everyone else's lunch trays were almost empty, I'd eaten a forkful of mac 'n' cheese before pushing away my tray.

"Lacey was ridic," Khloe said.

She, Clare, and I had been giving Lexa the details of the awful English class.

"I'm just glad that Taylor doesn't have lunch during

our period," I said. "That sounds so mean, but it would make things harder to have him in the room and want to sit with him but feel like I can't."

"Not because of Lacey, right?" Lexa asked. Her black curls were held away from her face with two rhinestone butterfly clips. The butterflies' red wings matched the reddish tint in Lexa's hair.

"Never," I said, shaking my head. "Lacey can pout and be mad at me all she wants, but it wouldn't make me ditch Tay. I was thinking about Drew. It would be awkward to have Taylor sit with us for lunch, and if he had it this period, I'd *want* him to."

Clare took a bite of pumpkin pie. "I told you that I had pre-algebra with him before lunch."

Khloe nodded so hard that I thought she'd bounce right off her seat.

"You dangled that in front of us, Clare Bryant, and that's all you said!" Khloe pretend-chastised her friend.

"We sat together," Clare said. "Our teacher was a few minutes late, so we talked a little." She smiled at me. "He talked about you, Lauren, and how coming here was the best thing that had ever happened to him."

"Did Taylor say he wants Lauren back?" Lexa asked.

"Yeah, did he?" Khloe asked.

"Guuuys. Taylor's not like that," I said. Then I shifted my eyes to Clare. "Well . . . what *did* he say?"

"Taylor was like you told us—totally cool. I asked him a bunch of questions about himself, what he liked to do for fun, et cetera, et cetera." Clare smiled.

I felt relieved, even though I knew Taylor wouldn't kiss and tell.

"I'm glad he had someone to hang out with during class," I said. "I know what it felt like to be the newbie."

For the rest of lunch my friends shared gossip, made me laugh, and helped take away the sting of Lacey's behavior.

"Sorry I missed you at lunch."

I finished putting my just-emptied tray on the rack and turned toward the familiar voice.

Drew, in a red crewneck sweater and jeans, leaned against the wall and smiled at me.

"Me too," I said, unable to hold back what I was sure was a silly grin. "I thought you might have switched lunch periods to hang with the cool people."

Drew laughed. "I tried that, but Ms. Utz said I *had* to have lunch this period. Major bummer."

I grinned. "Maybe I'll be lucky enough to catch you at the stable sometime."

"Hmmm. That might work out," Drew said. His blue eyes caught the light as he flicked them to me. "Or we could switch up our workouts if you're game."

Drew and I had been running together on mornings when we were free before school. We'd connected over our mutual love of jogging as a way to clear our heads.

"Try me, Adams." I folded my arms, giving him my best *bring it on* face.

"Instead of running tomorrow morning, what about swimming? The pool will be deserted, and it'll be a good change for our muscles."

"I'm in," I said. No hesitation. "I'm being wimpy, since it's barely November, but I'd rather go swim in a heated indoor pool than jog in the cold that early in the morning."

"Done." Drew smiled, flashing dimples in both cheeks.

I suddenly realized I'd gone from having my arms folded to hugging myself like a dork. Boys *never* had that effect on me. Until Drew.

"Cool. BBM me a time later?" I said.

"Sure thing. See you at riding." Drew smiled again before heading to the lunch line.

I waved and joined Khloe, Clare, and Lexa, who were waiting by the caf exit.

"Someone looks a little happier," Clare said, bumping me with her shoulder.

I had to force myself *not* to skip toward the door. "I just talked to Drew, and he was so great."

"Tell, tell!" Khloe said. "We're not leaving this cafeteria until you spill, LT."

"Mmm, *okay*," I said. "If you really want to know . . ."

Simultaneously my three friends shot me dirty looks.

I laughed. "Okay! He said he was sorry he'd missed our lunch period."

"Awww," Lexa said with a happy sigh.

The girls stared at me with wide, round eyes, waiting for me to finish my Boy Story.

"Then he asked if I wanted to shake up our usual morning runs."

Clare stopped mid-gloss, the pink wand hovering above her bottom lip. "Like how?"

"Like, Drew asked if I wanted to go *swimming* tomorrow morning instead of running."

Clare, Lexa, and Khloe let out ear-piercing squeals.

"Omigod! Laureeen!" Khloe said. She grabbed my forearm and fanned her face with her other hand.

"This. Is. Huge," Lexa said. "That's Drew's other thing. He has riding and he has swimming. He wants to introduce you to his other fave thing to do!"

"I know!" I said. "I'm so excited! I'm so glad I took swimming lessons when I was a kid. My mom made me go when I was little, and I *hated* it. The pool was always freezing, and the floaty arm things pinched my skin. But after I learned, my parents probably regretted it. I was always begging to go swimming."

"You guys," Clare started. She'd given up on glossing and had tucked the Ulta gloss back into her pocket. "I think you're forgetting one, oh I don't know, *tiny* thing."

I couldn't think of anything. . . . I stared at Khloe, then at Lexa. Both girls shook their heads at me.

Clare's cheeks went pink. She leaned closer to us. "You're going to see Drew . . . with his shirt off!"

OH, mon Dieu!

I clapped a hand over my mouth to keep a squeak from coming out. Lexa and Khloe, though, didn't even try.

"Omigod, omigod!" Lexa said. "We can't talk about this in here! Drew's getting his lunch. C'mon."

Linking arms, we all burst into giggles and scurried toward the door.

19

HELLO, GORGEOUS!

AFTER CLASS I HURRIED BACK TO MY DORM, alone, and went to change for my riding lesson. Khloe's advanced class wasn't until after mine, so she didn't have to rush back to Hawthorne. She'd gone to meet a group of friends from theater, and they were running lines for *Beauty and the Beast*.

Inside my room I dropped my backpack beside my desk and plugged my BlackBerry into the charger.

I slid out of my school clothes and went to the section of my closet that contained my riding clothes. Layers were key for today to stay warm. Tan breeches. Wool socks. Black tank top. A black-and-gray rugby-stripe sweater and a black toggle coat.

As I dressed, I thought about Khloe at practice. She'd

been prepping for her role as Belle ever since Riley had left campus. Khloe's theater rival had landed the coveted lead as Belle, and Khloe had been given the part of Mrs. Potts and was Riley's understudy. It had looked as though Riley would be the one to lead the drama club's fall production, until a few weeks ago. Without telling anyone, even her so-called best friend Clare, Riley had landed a role on a TV pilot shooting in New York City and had decided to leave Canterwood.

I had a gut feeling that Riley wouldn't be the successful actor she strived to be. She didn't care about acting like Khloe did. Khloe approached acting like she did riding—she cared about the craft, read a zillion books on the topic, and practiced. Riley, on the other hand, had only wanted to be a star. A celebrity. I knew from my time spent around girls like that on the A circuit, who wanted to be superstar riders without really loving the sport, that it could only take them so far.

I sat at my desk chair, lacing up my boots. On Khloe's message board she had *FIRST PERFORMANCE!!!* written in sparkly blue gel pen. The date? One week. Cliché nervous butterflies fluttered in my stomach for my best friend.

"Okay," I said aloud. "Time to get out of here."

I unplugged my phone, slipped it into my coat pocket, and shut our door behind me. I walked down the hallway, beautifully decorated for fall with pumpkins, fake leaves, and gourds on the tables. I peeked inside Hawthorne's dorm monitor Christina's office as I walked by. She was on the phone, sounding as if she was talking to a parent about Parents' Weekend activities.

That gave me a case of my own butterflies. In less than two weeks my parents and Becca would be on campus. I'd be showing them around, introducing them to my friends, and giving them a taste of Canterwood life.

My phone vibrated in my pocket, making me jump as I walked. I laughed aloud at myself for being such a dork. Navigating the campus courtyard was like walking the streets of bustling New York City. No one had noticed my silly freak-out, nor were they staring at me like I was a crazy person for laughing at myself.

I pulled my phone out of my pocket and checked the screen. There was a new BBM.

Taylor:

Survived first day. Um, u didn't tell me that I needed 2 prep 2 give up all free time bc of schoolwork!

I started down the gentle incline to the stable, typing as I walked.

Lauren:

Yay! ☺ I knew u'd make it, Tay. The hw scared me 2, but it (somehow!) becomes part of ur routine. U'll be blowing thru it soon.

Taylor is writing a message appeared.

Taylor:

Hope so. Thx 4 the confidence, Laur. ☺ What r u doing?

Lauren:

Walking 2 the stable. Riding lesson then back 2 room 4 hw. And I'll prob be helping Khloe run lines 4 the play.

Taylor:

Say hi to Whisper 4 me. Good luck @ ur lesson. I'm gonna start hw now bc I wanna b 100% sure I finish everything. Not giving Dad 1 reason 2 make me come home.

Lauren:

U've got this, Tay. If u need help, BBM me anytime. Ur not going 2 mess up and ur dad's not going to take u home. I won't let him. ☺

I reached the stable front and locked my phone. I went straight to the tack room, which was full of lower-grade and upper-class students. It took a minute for me to see an opening to squeeze through to grab Whisper's tack. I'd stored her grooming kit in the wooden trunk outside her stall so I'd have less to carry back and forth.

I scooted around riders in the aisles and deposited

Whisper's tack on her trunk. Lifting the ballerina-pink lead line from the hook next to her stall door, I peered inside.

"Hello, gorgeous!"

An automatic smile came to my face when my eyes landed on Whisper. She blinked at me with delicate lashes that framed her gorgeous dark-brown eyes. I opened the stall door and then slid it shut behind me. My boots sank into the clean, deep sawdust as I hurried to Whisper and threw my arms around her neck. One of the grooms had thrown one of Whisper's blankets across her back and secured the Velcro straps at her chest. The pink blanket matched her lead line.

"Chilly today, huh, baby?" I asked. "You're going to have fun during your lesson, and you'll forget all about being cold. I think we're going to be jumping today."

Mr. Conner had e-mailed my class last night and instructed us to meet him near the outside large arena.

"Hey, girlies!"

A voice carried over the neighboring stall.

"Hey, Lex," I called back. "Want to groom together?"

"Def."

We led our horses out of their stalls and into the aisle. Both of us scanned the stable for a spot roomy enough for four.

"There," I said, pointing to a spot where a dark-haired older guy untied a flea-bitten gray mare and led her down the aisle.

Lex and I, with Honor and Whisper in tow, scurried to grab the free ties. Lexa walked back to our stalls and grabbed both of our tack boxes.

She was unusually quiet as she took off Honor's royal-purple blanket. I undid Whisper's blanket, folding it but watching Lexa.

"You okay?" I asked. "You seemed really upbeat when you got here, and now you're really quiet."

Lexa's face was hidden as she brushed Honor's neck. She flicked the body brush over the bay's coat a few times before turning to me.

"Lauren, I'm sorry. I *hate* being in this position. I have to tell you something, but I want to protect you and *not* say anything. You're one of my closest friends, though, so I feel like I'm lying if I don't tell you."

"Lex, you're *really* scaring me," I said. I ducked under Whisper's neck and stood in front of my friend. "Whatever it is, I'm not going to be mad at you. I get your instinct to protect me, but I need to know."

"That's what Khloe and Clare said," Lexa said, her voice soft.

"You told them something before you even told me?" I asked. "Why?"

Both mares lifted their heads at my loud voice.

"No. *No*," Lexa said, shaking her head. "It's not like that at all. I swear. It's—" She stopped, and I stood motionless, staring at her.

"Lexa, please just tell me."

Lexa played with the bristles on Honor's body brush before looking up at me. "I had class with Clare last period today. Clare had to see Ms. Utz about a volunteer program she wants to do over Christmas break, and I went with her."

I nodded. "Okay."

"Taylor was waiting to see Ms. Utz too. We sat next to him and talked to him for, like, two seconds before Ms. Utz called him into her office. When he got up, his BlackBerry was on the seat. It must have been in his pocket or something and fallen out."

Whisper bumped my arm with her muzzle. She was doing the *hey Lauren don't forget I'm here* act. I rubbed her neck. "Please, *please* don't tell me that you guys went through his phone or something."

I regretted my words the second they left my mouth.

Lexa's eyes widened. "Of course not! Lauren, you know us better than that."

"Lex, I'm so sorry," I said. I reached out and touched her elbow. "I *do* know better, and I'm really sorry I said that."

Lexa gave me a tight smile. "Clare picked up Taylor's phone so no one else would grab it, and we were waiting for Taylor to come out. He got a text when he was inside. His phone wasn't locked, and the message was visible for a few seconds before the screen darkened."

His dad. Something's happening with Mr. Frost that Tay's hiding from me. I knew Taylor. Very well. So well that I'd been fighting the feeling that he'd been keeping something from me. I hadn't even admitted it to myself because I didn't want to think about what it might be. I'd chalked it up to Tay being nervous about Mr. Frost, since he'd been a little . . . *off* around me since day one. But now Lexa was about to confirm my worst fear.

"What did it say?" I asked. "I already know it was from his dad. Oh, poor Taylor. I'm going to have to find some way to talk to him about it. He must be so upset and—"

"Lauren, it wasn't his dad," Lexa cut in. Her caramel-and-mocha-colored eyes locked with mine. "It was Brielle. She wrote, 'I really miss you. You didn't call last night.'"

I was silent.

"Laur?" Lexa asked after a few long seconds. "Are you okay?"

I stepped forward and gently shook my friend's shoulders.

"Lexa Reed!" I said. "You scared me! I thought it was something really serious!"

Confusion was all over Lexa's face. "Isn't it? Taylor got a text from another girl. One of your best friends. He didn't call her last night."

"Lex, I'm sorry you were stressing over that. But it's nothing. Bri and Taylor are friends. They hung out all the time, and I know they text. I'm sure Bri just asked Taylor to actually 'call her' last night, and he didn't for some reason."

Slowly Lexa nodded. "Oh. I didn't know they were friend-friends. I'm so sorry! I feel really dumb right now."

"Hey, don't," I said. "I meant it—I'm sorry *you* got worried. You're such a good friend that you were looking out for me. It's not as though I talk about Bri and Taylor's friendship for you to have known that they are close. Please don't feel silly about anything."

Lexa smiled. "Okay. Thanks, Laur. I've learned my lesson about reading other people's texts. It'll never happen again."

I bumped Lexa's arm with my elbow. "Never say never.

I can't promise I won't read texts if I somehow stumble onto Lacey's phone."

Lexa and I started laughing and went back to grooming our horses. Within minutes just being in Whisper's presence made me forget about everything else going on in my life. It was my horse and me.

20

WHOSE GUT
TO TRUST?

MY INSTINCT THAT WE WOULD BE JUMPING today was right on. Mr. Conner, Mike, and Doug added the last few oxers to a moderately difficult course in the largest outdoor arena while Drew, Cole, Lexa, Clare, and I warmed up our horses.

Whisper seemed happy to be out of the stable. I felt a little guilty that I hadn't spent nearly the amount of time with her as I normally did, but last week had been insane. I'd barely had time to brush my teeth. I looked down from Whisper's saddle at her shiny gray coat and felt all the more gracious toward Mike and Doug for grooming her when I couldn't and for keeping her company.

"All right, class," Mr. Conner called. "Line up in front of me, please."

We guided our horses to a stop in front of Mr. Conner. Whisper chewed her snaffle bit, ready to get out of line and start jumping.

"Each of you will take the course that has been set up for you. After your ride your classmates and I will critique your form."

Clare and I exchanged *eek!* glances.

"And to keep you informed, I will be away this weekend. I'll be traveling with the eighth-grade advanced team to an out-of-state show. So, if you need to reach me for any urgent reason that cannot wait, my cell number is in the student directory. I'll send you all an e-mail with my number just in case you can't find your directory."

A year ago I never thought I'd think it, but now I couldn't wait until I was one of the riders traveling out of town. I knew Sasha was on the eighth-grade advanced team, and I wondered how she'd do. Likely there would be a bunch of blue ribbons coming home with her. I'd have to wish her luck (in my head) later.

"Lauren, I'd like to see you and Whisper up first," Mr. Conner said. "Please dismount, walk the course to get a feel for the distance, and then give it a try. There aren't any switchbacks or anything tricky. Instead I added more combinations, and there are more jumps than most of your previous courses."

Following Mr. Conner's instructions, I dismounted and handed Whisper's reins to Lexa. While I walked the course, Mr. Conner talked to everyone about the importance of walking a course and how to get the most of it.

When I felt satisfied that I knew how many strides I'd be asking for between jumps, I rejoined the group, took Whisper's reins, and remounted. This course was longer than usual, with fourteen jumps, but I felt that Whisper and I could handle it. All we could do was our best.

"Whenever you're ready," Mr. Conner said.

I took a breath and turned Whisper away from the other horses and riders. Mr. Conner guided them out of the arena, and I halted Whisper at the arena entrance. Even though we weren't being timed, our time would have started the second Whisper had set foot in the large practice space.

I squeezed my legs against Whisper's sides, asking for a trot, and quickly let her out into a slow canter. I kept a firm grip on the reins, so she didn't get too excited before the first jump and rush. We cleared a simple white vertical and, a few strides later, jumped a higher vertical. I let Whisper gain a little speed as she moved to the third jump, an oxer. This one didn't have a particularly large spread, and she cleared it easily. But there was another oxer immediately after, and Whisper dug her heels into the ground as she pushed off to clear the wider spread. I held my breath for a second, afraid she'd clip the rail with her back hooves, but we landed cleanly, and the rail stayed in place.

I smiled, but quickly refocused. We had a long way to go.

Whisper took a higher vertical, bright orange poles, as if she was stepping over a ground pole. I did a half halt and slowed her before a triple combination, the blue-and-white rails looking a little daunting. Whisper cleared the first third of the jump, took one stride, vaulted into the air and landed on the other side of the middle combo, and with one more stride lifted off the ground to clear the final part of the triple combination.

We cantered away, and all the poles had stayed in their cups. *Yes*! I thought. *I want to kiss Whisper's muzzle right now!* I was so giving her extra, *extra* treats when we finished. Mr. Conner gave us several strides and a short half turn in the arena before Whisper jumped a plastic wall that looked just like stone.

After the wall, she cleared a vertical and an oxer and

we cantered toward a faux water jump. The tarp had a decent spread, so I let Whisper quicken her canter. She flicked her ears back and forth, weaving a little. Water jumps weren't her favorite. Fake water or not.

I squeezed my legs tighter around her sides and urged her forward, letting her know that running out on the jump or refusing weren't options. As Whisper prepared to launch over the tarp, I felt a tiny ripple through her muscles as she shuddered a little. I gave her more rein and tapped my boots against her sides, encouraging her to keep moving. Whisper landed with her back hooves inches away from the tarp. That was my girl!

The rest of the course was easy. We conquered another vertical, an oxer as the twelfth jump, a high vertical, and finished with a triple combination.

When Whisper cantered away from the course, I switched my reins to my right hand and petted her neck. I didn't care what critiques I was about to receive. *I* was more than proud of my horse, and in my eyes she'd given me the perfect ride and put her whole heart into it. I couldn't have asked for more.

21

NOW OR NEVER

WHEN MY ALARM WENT OFF AT FIVE ON
Wednesday morning, I had already been awake for what
seemed like hours. Drew and I were *finally* going to see
each other and swim. The thought of seeing Drew and
working out with him made me too excited to sleep! I
rolled onto my side and stopped my vibrating phone. I
slid out of my warm bed and padded to my desk chair,
where I'd laid out my clothes for the morning.

I grabbed my clothes and headed for the bathroom,
stopping in the doorway. On the other side of the dark
room, Khloe was still asleep. She was buried under a
pile of purple-and-hot-pink flannel sheets and a matching comforter. She had an arm over her rainbow unicorn
Pillow Pet, Sparkles.

Good, I thought. *She helped me so much last night.*

I shut the bathroom door behind me and turned on the light. The night before last Khloe had helped me pick the perfect I-just-pulled-this-out-of-my-closet outfit to wear on my way to the pool. She'd also helped me pick my bathing suit. I'd only brought one when I'd come to Canterwood, and it didn't feel like *the* suit I wanted to wear to swim with Drew.

Khloe had helped me search online for a new suit. We each used our own computers and looked through four stores. Khloe had Delia's and Target, and I searched Macy's and a Brooklyn sportswear store where I'd bought swimsuits before.

We'd each picked three suits and then showed each other our choices. Instantly we'd agreed that Khloe had picked The Suit—a bright pink tankini with purple ruched hipster bottoms. I'd scored on the price, since it *was* November, and had saved enough money to pay to have the suit shipped overnight. I'd tried it on yesterday, and it had fit perfectly. A bathing suit wasn't all that I'd need to wear, though. I had to have *something* on to get from Hawthorne to the gym.

Khloe had gone through my closet and had pulled together an outfit in under two minutes. It was a game she and I had unintentionally created last week, when I'd helped Khlo find an outfit in a hurry. Now, whenever one of us wanted help from the other, we tried to form a complete outfit in two minutes or less.

Khloe's choices were perfect. She'd picked sapphire-blue velour Xhilaration pants and a matching hoodie. A long-sleeve white thermal shirt and my gray-and-lilac Pumas completed the look. Once I'd slid into my suit and finished dressing, I twisted my hair back with a clip.

I reached for my Yes to Cucumbers face wipes and pulled out one of the moist towelettes. I wiped away the sleepiness from my eyes and the oily shine that had accumulated on my T-zone overnight. The fresh scent was invigorating and calming to my skin all at once. I rubbed a pearl-size amount of lotion onto my face and double-checked the mirror for any blemishes that might have popped up overnight. I squinted but didn't see anything. I took the clip out of my hair, shaking out my locks.

I brushed my hair and quickly put it in a French braid, leaving a few wisps of hair free. I didn't want to spend much time on my hair, since it was going to get wet anyway in a few minutes.

"Okay," I said to my reflection in the mirror. "It's now or never. Just go."

Khloe had flipped onto her other side and was facing the wall when I shut and locked our door behind me. Hawthorne was silent. I tiptoed down the hall and eased open the entrance door.

Freezing air felt like it pricked any exposed skin when I stepped outside. I hurried down the steps and broke into a jog. I wanted to warm up my body *and* get to the gym faster. I ran around the empty courtyard, passed the empty tennis courts, and jogged around the covered outdoor pool.

I slowed to a walk when I saw Drew. His shock of black hair was a little tousled in the morning.

"Hey, you copied me. You're in Puma sneakers too," I called to him.

Drew laughed and looked down at his tracksuit. He'd chosen a black Puma jacket, matching pants with a white stripe down the side, and a white T-shirt. And Puma sneakers.

"It does look like we called each other and decided what to wear before we went out, doesn't it?" Drew asked.

"Totally," I said. "If our bathing suits match, though, I'm going to feel *really* ripped off."

We both laughed, and Drew pulled open the door for me. I stepped inside the pool area and let out an appreciative sigh for the warm air.

"This is a way better idea than trying not to turn into icicles by jogging," I said.

Drew unzipped his jacket and tossed it onto the lowest row of bleachers. "For sure. I'm still going to make you jog with me, though, even when there are three feet of snow on the ground."

I tugged off my hoodie and put a hand on my hip. "Excuse me? I never promised to run in the snow!"

Drew kicked off his sneakers, grinning. "Fine. I won't ask you to run. We'll go snowshoeing."

I stared at him. "*Snowshoeing?* You mean that 'sport' where people trek through the snow for miles with giant tennis rackets strapped to their feet?"

"Yep," Drew said simply. The pool water reflected in his eyes and made them look extra blue.

"Okay, Adams. Game on. Today, swimming. Next month, snowshoeing."

Drew, laughing, headed for the far end of the pool. I watched him walk away shirtless and in long black swim trunks.

Um. Whoa.

My bare feet felt stuck to the tile floor. I was in my bathing suit too, and Drew had made it so easy to get undressed in front of him. It had been something I'd worried about since he'd first suggested swimming. I'd been swimming at the lake at home plenty of times with a group of friends from school or riders from Briar Creek, and there were always guys. But I'd never swum alone with a boy before. Part of me had thought I'd get into the pool *with* my pants and shirt on, but that thought had disappeared the moment I'd met Drew outside.

I bent my right knee and touched the water with my other foot. *Parfait!*

"You're not getting in at *that* end, are you, Towers?" Drew called. He was suspended over the pool on a low diving board.

"You're diving in?" I asked. "Is it deep enough?"

Drew dropped his teasing act and nodded. "It's just over twelve feet deep at this end, so it's safe. Don't try to dive in anywhere else, though."

"I won't, trust me." I walked along the edge of the pool toward Drew. "I don't know how to dive."

"Do you want to learn?" Drew turned, walked off the board, and stopped in front of me. "I could teach you."

"I'd love to be able to dive. But my friends have been trying to teach me for years, and I never learned how. I always end up doing a belly flop or jumping straight in."

Drew waved his hand. "Belly flops end this morning.

By the time we leave the gym, you'll be diving."

A little bit of nerves pulsed through me. "You sure? You came to work out this morning, not play swimming coach."

Drew smiled. It was the gentle, soft smile that soothed my nerves. "I'm sure, Laur." He held out his hand to me. I placed my still chilled hand into his warm one. Tingles! He led me in the direction of the deep end of the pool. "I promise that you'll be able to add 'diver' to your list of skills once we're done."

I reached for my throat to play with my necklace. I was surprised when it wasn't there. Then I remembered that I'd taken off all my jewelry before coming this morning.

"We're not going to start on the diving board," Drew said. "We'll start from the edge of the pool, and I'll do a couple of dives so you can watch my body formation first. Then you can try. Okay?"

"Okay," I said.

Drew stood straight, raising both arms above his head. "See how my arms are against my ears?"

"Yes."

"That's how you should be. So you'll stand straight, turn to the pool, and bend at your torso."

"That's the part where I always mess up," I said,

blushing a little. "It always feels like I'm falling into the pool, and it feels like my instincts kick in and my body wants to stop it. That's why I always end up belly flopping or not even trying at all and just jumping right in."

Drew lowered his arms and looked at me. "I understand the fear of falling. Believe me. Even though my *brain* knows there's water for me to sink into, there's always still a tiny voice in my head telling me, 'Diving? That's one of the dumbest things I've ever heard!'"

His story made me laugh. "Glad I'm not the only one."

"You're not. I promise. And, Laur? I'm sorry for bringing this up, but I wonder if diving will help you in some way with your accident."

I stilled, memories of that awful day flashing a million times per second in front of me.

"How do you think it could help?" I asked, my voice soft.

Drew was so close to me, I could smell whatever minty toothpaste he'd used this morning.

"It might help you get over your fear of falling. You've already conquered your fear of falling from horseback by riding again, but who knows? Maybe something different—another fear of falling conquered—would help too."

Slowly I shook my head.

"Did I say something wrong?" Drew asked. His voice was thick with concern.

"Oh, no! Not at all. I was just thinking how . . . ," I paused, realizing what I was about to say and hoping I didn't freak him out. "I was thinking about how lucky I am to have you in my life. I'm so, so happy we're together."

Drew smiled—a grin that showed off all of his white teeth—and reached out to squeeze my hand. "I think I'm the lucky one. You tell me you're happy that I'm in your life *after* we're finished with diving lessons."

Giggling, I nodded. We got to work, not wasting any precious seconds of the morning. I watched Drew perform several dives from the floor, and he taught me what to look for, exactly how to arch my back, when to lean over the water, and when it was time to push off with my toes.

My first "dive" was a belly flop, and I caused giant waves to ripple through the pool. Drew made me get out and dive again. And again. And again.

Dripping wet, I walked the well-traveled length to the deep end of the pool. Drew, treading water in the pool, nodded at me. "C'mon, Lauren. You can do it."

His words were in my ears as I placed my arms above

my head, touching them to my ears. I bent forward slightly, and *something* kicked in to tell me now was the time to push off the floor with my toes. I bounced off the floor, trying to keep my feet and hands somewhat together. My fingertips hit the water first, followed by my head, torso, and legs. I kicked underwater, driving myself a few feet deeper, then turned right side up and swam to the top.

I spun around, treading water, and faced Drew. His expression was blank.

My stomach fell a little. *This* was the moment when he realized I wasn't teachable.

"I'm sorry," I said. "I know it wasn't perfect. I mean, it wasn't even close to good. I'm so sorry I wasted your time this morning. We never have to swim together again, and I—"

"Lauren!" Drew half shouted, interrupting me.

He swam over to me and treaded water in front of me. "You *dove*! You dove! You took everything I taught you and applied it to your form and technique. No lie—that was a great dive!"

"What?" I treaded water, but felt as though I could stay afloat on my own.

"I'm so proud of you!"

Words couldn't describe how I felt. But something

else could. I wrapped my arms over Drew's shoulders, and before I could do it, *he kissed me.*

Even in the warm pool, all the hair stood up on my arms. His soft lips on mine made me feel like I'd never been kissed—at least not like this. I forgot to tread water for a second, holding on to him, then remembered I'd probably drown us both if I stopped.

We pulled apart after a few seconds, and I looked into his eyes. He had this little-boy grin on his face.

"It seemed appropriate that our first kiss was in the pool," I said.

"It would seem appropriate that our second kiss would be too," Drew said.

Leaning forward, I kissed my then-without-a-doubt boyfriend for the second time that morning.

22

ON MY NERVES

ONCE RIDING LESSONS WERE OVER, I FELT like I had nowhere to go. I didn't want to go back to my room yet. Khloe would be there, and Clare had started to apologize since Monday, but I'd been avoiding her.

I went to the first place I thought of—the courtyard. It was empty, and I sat on a stone bench, happy for the quiet. The only sounds were of students off in the distance, an occasional whinny, birds chirping as they flew overhead—all noises that blended into the background.

I don't know what he's hiding, I just know that it's something.

The words Clare had spoken during the warm-up of our lesson rolled around in my brain.

Ugh, I told myself. *Think of something—anything else.*

I thought about today's fashion class with Cole. Since

the play would begin on Monday, our schedules had changed, and we had fashion class daily. No complaints from me! Cole and I were hard at work creating the best Lumière costume to ever grace the Canterwood theater's stage.

We'd decided to keep the concept close to the movie version of Lumière and not to mess with something that was such a beloved classic.

I blinked, my eyelids feeling a little heavy. In addition to fashion class, practices for glee club were more frequent than normal. We were meeting to practice a song for our parents to show them what we'd learned in glee club. I was a little nervous to perform in front of my family, but also insanely excited. I loved glee, and I hoped Mom, Dad, and Becca saw that when I sang.

I pulled my charcoal peacoat tighter around me. The temperature was dropping, as the sun had already started to set in the late afternoon.

I wasn't being blinded by my friendship with Taylor—Clare had to be wrong. It was annoying that she'd dragged Khloe into the Taylor's keeping-a-secret theory and even worse that Khloe was starting to agree with her. I knew Taylor better than anyone else here, and I had to trust my gut. Tay wasn't hiding anything bad. He wasn't that kind of guy. Everything I knew about him screamed that whatever Clare perceived he was hiding was something I already knew: Mr. Frost.

Taylor wasn't the type of guy to talk every time his dad did something that made his life harder. Even though Tay and I were still friends, he'd stopped sharing as much of his dad drama when we'd broken up last summer. Just because we weren't together didn't mean Taylor couldn't talk to me. And he knew that. So why was I sitting on a cold bench trying to shake Clare and Khloe's concerns?

My phone chimed, and I pulled it out of my pocket. There was a new BBM.

Ana:

Hey, Laur. How's everything?

It was like my Union bestie had ESP. Ana knew when I needed her.

Lauren:

It's SO crazy that u wrote me right now. I'm sitting outside mulling over some Tay stuff. Rlly glad 2 hear from u.

A few seconds passed before Ana wrote back.

Ana:

What kind of Taylor stuff?

Lauren:

Nothing major. Khloe and my friend Clare think he's hiding something.

Ana:

Do u think he is?

Lauren:

No way. It's TAYLOR. I mean, I have this weird feeling that he's not telling me something. But I rlly think it's abt his dad and T doesn't want 2 overshare and make it awkward btwn us or something.

I quickly sent a second message.

Lauren:

Not that it would. T can always talk 2 me. We're friends.

Ana:

Lauren, I'm sorry u think something's off. I wish I knew the right thing 2 do.

It took Ana forever to type that message. The *Ana is writing a message* note started and stopped flashing about half a dozen times before I got the BBM. *She's probably busy now,* I thought.

Lauren:

What do u mean? The right thing 2 do? Like whether or not 2 ask T 2 talk 2 me?

Ana:

Yeah. Asking him 2 tell u the truth . . .

I waited while she typed her next message.

Ana:

I'm so sorry, but I have 2 go. I know I wrote u and I'm a bad friend for ending our convo when u r having a crisis.

Lauren:

Ur not a bad friend, A! And it's not a crisis—rlly. Just thinking abt what 2 do next. I'm just glad u said hi. Skype soon?

Ana:

Definitely. Ur the best, LT. Love u!

Lauren:

Love u 2! Xx

I exited out of BBM, locked my phone, and put it back in my pocket. I wasn't going to chase down Taylor and bombard him with questions. If he wanted or needed to talk to me, he would.

Boot heels tapped on the cobblestone, and someone paused behind me. Inwardly I sighed. It had to be Khloe or Clare wanting to talk. I loved them both, but I *really* wanted to drop the whole Taylor thing.

I stayed still, my back to whoever it was, and the footsteps approached and I stared at the unfamiliar paddock boots that walked past me, then turned and stopped in front of me.

I looked up and my breath caught. I'd only read about

people's breaths actually *catching*. It hadn't seemed real—until now!

I stared at a face I'd seen a thousand times.

On DVDs.

In photos at Briar Creek.

On the school Website.

In the newspaper.

I stared at a girl I'd heard about a thousand times.

From Kim, my old riding instructor.

From Ana and Brielle.

From Mr. Conner.

From my new friends.

From my parents.

From riders at my old stable.

A million thoughts zoomed through my brain as I sat there, frozen.

What is she going to say?

Why has she stopped in front of me?

Does she even know who I am?

Am I sitting on *her* bench by mistake?

My outfit! Do I look like a mess in my coat, lilac sweater, and my dark jeans tucked into my boots?

I was staring at The Legend. The superstar graduate of Briar Creek. The rider I wanted to be like more than anyone in the world. The girl who had left Union and *made* it. An equestrian who had made it possible for pre-Canterwood me to even dare dream of attending this school.

Sasha Silver had stopped in front of me.

Oh, mon Dieu.

23

THE LEGENDARY
SUPERSTAR

"HI," SASHA SAID.

The older girl looked every bit as polished as her reputation. I stared *and* stared, taking in every detail about her. Sasha wore army-green breeches with black paddock boots and a wool coat. A tan sweater peeked out from the coat, and she had a horseshoe-shaped ring on her right hand.

"I'm Sasha Silver," she continued.

It was my turn to speak, but I didn't know if I could.

"I know," I said, my voice soft. "You're *the* Sasha Silver from Union. From Briar Creek. It's so nice to meet you."

Suddenly I felt like I should be standing. I jumped off the bench and stood. I stretched out my hand to Sasha. Hopefully, she didn't think I was weirdly formal, but shaking her hand felt like the right move.

I smiled when Sasha immediately stuck out her hand and shook mine. She eyed the bench, and I moved down to one end and Sasha sat at the opposite. We both turned so we faced each other.

"And I know you, too," Sasha said.

No way! Don't freak out! I said to myself. But !!!!!! Sasha knew my name! I smiled, fighting the urge to (a) dance, (b) BBM all of my friends, and (c) take a video of this moment so I'd believe it was real.

"I came to visit Briar Creek a long time ago," Sasha said. "I saw you jumping in a field. Kim told me about you and how great you were."

I blushed. A deep, *deep* red. "Not even close to you," I said. "Kim never stops talking about you. She uses your story as a way to encourage all of the riders at Briar Creek to look ahead and go for what we want."

Sasha, smiling, looked at her lap and then back at me.

"And you wanted to come to Canterwood?"

I nodded, playing with an edge of the case of my phone. "More than anything," I said. I gave her a tiny smile. "It's terrifying, but I have to try."

Sasha looked at me like she was studying me. I felt like I saw a million thoughts flash through her brain as she got a far-off look in her eyes. I wondered if she was thinking about her own journey. From everything I'd heard, Sasha's experience from Briar Creek to Canterwood hadn't been without ups and downs, but that made it all the more inspiring.

Sasha reached into her coat pocket and pulled out her BlackBerry.

"Here," she said. She held her phone out to me. "Put your number in my phone. Text me if you need anything, get lost, overwhelmed—whatever. You can talk to me anytime."

I grinned like an idiot. Getting Sasha Silver's number was like I'd gotten an A-list celeb's number. "Really?" I asked.

Sasha nodded, still holding out the phone.

"That's so nice of you," I said. "You have no idea how much less nervous that makes me feel."

I added myself as a contact to Sasha's address book. It took me three times as long to type the message—my fingers kept hitting all the wrong keys because they were shaking.

Sasha took her phone when I offered it back to her. My own phone beeped with a text from Sasha. Now I had her number.

"Good," she said, pulling a Lip Smackers from her

pocket. "And seriously. Anytime." She applied a coat of shiny, berry-tinted Dr Pepper gloss. I smiled to myself— the rumors of Sasha's lip gloss addiction were *definitely* true.

Sasha smiled, gave me a small wave, and headed out of the courtyard.

I forced myself to sit on the bench until I was a thousand percent sure that Sasha was gone. Then I stood and hurried to Hawthorne at a flat-out run to tell Khloe everything.

After I told Khloe about meeting The Famous Sasha Silver and we analyzed every detail of the conversation, Khloe got a serious look on her face.

"Laur, I want to apologize about the Taylor sitch," Khloe said.

We were sitting cross-legged on our fluffy carpet, facing each other.

"I talked to Clare, and we both agreed we were totally wrong," Khloe continued. "You know Taylor better than us, and we should have listened to you. I trust you implicitly, and I should have trusted your instincts. I'm sorry."

I looked into Khloe's brown eyes and saw the regret. I couldn't hold this against her.

"Khloe, wow," I said. "Thank you. Of course I forgive you and Clare. You're my roommate and best friend—I know you were only looking out for me. Clare and I have gotten a lot closer too, and she only had good intentions."

I reached out and touched Khloe's knee. She was cozy in black leggings with a stripe of cheetah print down each side. She'd found the leggings and an off-the-shoulder terry-cloth sweater at Deb online a few weeks ago.

Khloe smiled. A *huge* smile. "Omigod, LT. I'm so glad we're okay! I hate it when things are off between us! Wheeew!" She let out a giant sigh, flopping onto her back.

I giggled. "It's not funny, but I know what you mean. It sticks with me every second when we're fighting or things aren't right with our friendship. I think it's an extra-stressful time right now."

Khloe, still lying with her legs stretched in front of her just beside me, propped herself up on her elbows. "Tell me about it."

"We've got," I started, holding up a hand to count, "Parents' Weekend. A play. A glee club performance for the families. Riding lessons. Tons of schoolwork. Did I mention families?"

We giggled, and I held one palm up like a high five and

on the other hand just my thumb to give her a high six.

"Six things," I said. "And these are only the *B-I-G* things."

"Oh God," Khloe said, dropping back onto the rug. "Don't even try to count all the little things. You'll run out of fingers *and* toes."

I took a deep breath. I needed some calming tea. Maybe some of the Celestial Seasonings Honey Vanilla Chamomile that Mom had sent me last week.

"We need to do something, I don't know, *bonding*," Khloe said. A mischievous smile played on her lips. "Agree?"

"Most definitely. What do you have in mind?" I grinned.

"Oh, maybe a little thing called . . . online shopping?" Khloe sat up, staring at me and wiggling her eyebrows.

"*Ooh la la!* Grab your laptop!"

We got up, grabbed our computers, and lay on our stomachs across my bed. The need for calming tea completely disappeared.

"I think," Khloe said, "we need new socks. Not the boring white ones, but awesome ones for fall that act as accessories. What do you think?"

"I love that idea," I said. "We could keep them in a bin and share like we do with everything else."

"Yes!" Khloe said, shimmying her shoulders.

"It's so funny that you said socks, because I've been looking at the *coolest* socks online the past couple of days. I found the ultimate never-shopping-anywhere-else Website. It's going down as an EBT." I frowned. "Well, socks aren't *beauty*, technically, so I guess we need a new category."

"EST!" Khloe said.

"Essential style trick!" we said simultaneously.

Giggling, I opened Firefox and pulled up the Website. "Look. At. It." I said. "I've been trying to figure out a way to justify a huge charge on my credit card as an 'emergency,' but I think seeing 'Sock Dreams' as the charge will ruin my defense."

Khloe grinned. "Lucky for us, we have some cash in our checking accounts."

"*Exactly.* Check these out."

I showed Khloe the home page of Sock Dreams's Website. Then we got lost in socks. Ankle socks. Knee-high socks. Over-the-knee socks. Toe socks. Socks with rainbows. Argyle. Stripes. Fall patterns. Winter shades.

"Let's shop for LT socks first," Khloe said. "Then Khloe socks."

"Deal," I said.

Almost an hour later, I had an overflowing cart. Khloe and I had added every single pair of socks we liked, promising we'd cut socks before I checked out.

"Okay, I have to go through my cart, narrow it down, and check out," I said. "If I don't stop now, I'll never finish homework. Help me choose!"

Khloe put on her serious face. "Khloe Kinsella at your service."

It took us half an hour to settle on five pairs that I loved and Khloe fawned over: Extraordinary Harvest Rainbow Thigh-Highs (*parfait* to keep me warm during fall, and the colors—pomegranate, burnt orange, and plum, among others—were in for the season), Angora Faux Zipper Knee-Highs (gray with red tops and chic zipper detail), Confetti Kneesocks (ivory with army-green top and *très* cute polka dots), Cotton Argyle Tights (I'd chosen gray, black, and purple colors), and Peacock Feather Knee-Highs (black with a metallic-gold-and-turquoise peacock feather).

I let out a happy sigh once I'd checked out.

"I'm going to *so* be bugging Christina about the mail!" I said. "I wish we could snap our fingers and make the order appear right now."

"If online shopping worked that way, it would be sooo

bad," Khloe said, shaking her head. "I'd be broke, and you'd have to stage an intervention and force me to go to Shopaholics Anonymous meetings!"

We laughed.

"Seriously," Khloe said. "Total score, LT. Now . . . we're about to double our new collection!"

She turned her laptop screen in my direction. "My turn! Help me choose five."

"And *this* is why it's amaze to have a best friend and roomie that you can share clothes with," I said.

Khloe and I high-fived. I closed my laptop lid and leaned toward her computer. Together we browsed the Website for Khloe-like socks.

As we shopped, I let out a silent breath of relief that Khloe and I were okay again. I wasn't me without my best friend.

24

OUI, BE OUR GUEST!

MONDAY EVENING I SETTLED INTO MY SEAT at the theater. Opening night for *Beauty and the Beast* had sold out. I'd checked. Three times. I'd thought about Khloe all day and had only seen her after classes when I was changing for riding. She'd been excused from her lesson for the day, because her drama teacher wanted KK rested and to have plenty of time to get to the theater for makeup and costume.

Pre-performance Khloe was a side of her I'd never seen. She'd been *terrified*.

"Lauren," she had said hours ago. "I think I'm going to puke. I can't do this!"

"Khlo, yes you can. You *are* Belle." I pulled my room-mate away from the center of the room, where she was pacing a hole in the floor, and gently pushed her into her desk chair.

"You know *every* line in the play. Not just your lines but everyone's! You could probably recite all of *Beauty* backward." I crouched down and looked into my roomie's worried eyes.

"But I didn't get the role of Belle. I was cast as Mrs. Potts. Riley was supposed to be Belle! There had to be a reason why I wasn't cast as the lead, and it had something to do with me not being good enough."

"Khloe." My voice was firm. "You're more than good enough. You're right—Riley did get the role, but you were always the understudy. We'll never know why you weren't cast as the lead, and we could spend hours trying to guess. But know what?"

"What?" Khloe asked in a small voice.

"You *are* Belle now. I've run lines with you. I've seen you practice. I wouldn't lie to you and say 'Oh, Khloe, you're going to be amazing!' if I didn't think it was true. I'm being one hundred percent honest. I promise."

"Really?" Khloe's heaving chest started to slow, and color began to return to her face.

"Promise on our BFFness. I'm going to be in the audience tonight and every single night, silently cheering you on. You're a great actress, Khloe Kinsella. I can't wait to see you bring Belle to life."

A flutter of the red velvet curtain pulled me out of the memory. I'd gotten Khloe calmed down and had her laughing and back to Old Khloe by the time I'd left for my riding lesson. I'd lucked out that Mr. Conner had spent today's session teaching from a chapter in our horse manual instead of having us do flat work or jumping.

My intermediate class had spent the session covering a topic I thankfully knew—conformation. When I'd been called on to point out a conformation fault on a sketch of a horse on a piece of paper that Mr. Conner had given each of us, I'd answered the question right.

The theater kept filling as the seconds ticked down to the start of the play. Under my seat was a surprise for Khloe—a bouquet of daisies and baby's breath that I'd ordered online from the local florist. I'd managed to hide them from her all day by stashing them in one of the common room cupboards, and I couldn't wait to give them to her when the play ended.

The seat to my right was one of the few empty spots. It belonged to Cole, and he and I had bought tickets during lunch and made sure we had seats together.

I pulled my phone from my purse, turned it on silent,

and opened Chatter. I typed a quick update. *LaurBell: Abt 2 watch KK give a Tony-worthy performance as Belle! Très excited!* ☺

A familiar laugh cut through the talk in the theater. I didn't glance up as I put away my phone. *Do not look*, I told myself. But my body didn't listen to the warning voice. I glanced up, and two rows ahead Lacey sat with her friends. She was twisted around in her seat and chatting with someone in the row behind her. Her eyes met mine, and her mouth twisted into a fake smile. Lacey rolled her eyes, looking at me to make sure I'd seen her, then focused her attention back on the girl she was talking to.

"*That* was beyond tacky."

Cole slid in front of me and sank into the cushy seat next to me, sliding out of his coat.

"You mean Lacey?" I asked.

"Um, yeah. The girl's embarrassing herself so much. This whole 'Lauren's got two hotties after her' talk is so old. No one's even listening to her anymore. It's like she's talking to herself."

I shook my head. "People *are* listening. Don't pretend you haven't noticed that almost every girl in our grade won't talk to me anymore and is suddenly BFFs with Lacey."

It was Cole's turn for an eye roll. He brushed his light-brown hair off his forehead.

"All of those brainwashed girls are going to be *incredibly* embarrassed when they realize they'd ever listened to Lacey in the first place." Cole's voice rose and was tinged with anger. "They're going to remember how much they like you, and they're going to either flood you with apologies or be so embarrassed that they try to be your friends and pretend nothing ever happened."

I smiled. "Cole, you're the best. Thank you."

"Just telling you the truth."

I tipped my chin in Lacey's direction. "My truth is that I don't want to spend Khloe's night talking about her."

"So agree. Tonight's exciting for you and me, too!"

"I haven't forgotten that all day! We're actually going to see a costume *we* created and made, onstage in a real play."

Cole's green eyes were wide. "I'm so making sure I get backstage after to get a picture with Lumière."

"I know it's not the first time we'll see the costume on someone, but it's different because this isn't a costume fitting or a dress rehearsal. It's opening night, and students who aren't part of the play's production are going to see something you and I made!"

Cole grinned, nodding.

The lights dimmed and I swallowed. Hard. Every bit of my body felt electric. Like if I moved, I'd create static on the red seat and get shocked. I wasn't worried about Khloe, but I was still nervous. I wanted the play to run smoothly from the first line to the last. I'd watched Khloe give a flawless performance during a rehearsal, and I knew she'd do it tonight and every night the play ran.

I crossed my fingers and whispered, "Break a leg, Khlo."

The play began, and when Khloe appeared, in Belle's first costume, I almost stood and cheered. Khloe's blond hair was in a cap, and she wore a brown wig in a ponytail tied back with a ribbon. The blue ribbon matched Belle's dress.

Cole reached over and squeezed my arm. I smiled at him in the dim light and became transfixed by the actors onstage. Khloe Kinsella disappeared and *became* Belle. I didn't see my bubbly blond roommate anymore. I watched a book-loving small-town girl fight for her father's freedom, be held captive by a beast, and soon, fall in love.

25

TAKE A BOW

THE LIGHTS WENT UP AND THE ACTORS FILED onto the stage. I wiped tears from my cheeks as the cast joined hands and bowed. I leaped to my feet, with Cole right beside me, and clapped as hard as I could. My hands stung, and I whistled.

The entire cast had been *parfait*. I'd laughed, cried, and even sung along in my head to the songs I knew from watching the Disney movie version of the play.

Cole and I had grabbed each other's hands when Lumière had appeared onstage. There, for everyone to see, was a candelabra costume that Cole and I had created during fashion class. Cole and I had Googled dozens of images of Lumière, both from the Disney movie and from productions put on, from a high school in California to a college in England. We had pricked our fingers countless times with sewing needles, cut fabric the wrong size, and sketched dozens of bad ideas—but all of that disappeared when we saw our creation onstage.

Darren, the actor who played Lumière, had his face painted eggshell white to match the gauzy fabric Cole and I had used to create the tall headpiece. The "candle" parts of Lumière were made of light fabric so it wouldn't be too heavy for Darren's head or his arms. Ms. Snow had helped us stuff a portion of fabric with cotton and drape it over the front of the headpiece so it looked like melting wax.

For the wicks on Darren's head and hands, we'd twisted together black pipe cleaners and stuck them into Styrofoam that filled plastic plant pots. The pots had been green, but we'd spray-painted them gold. Inside we'd staple-gunned handles for Darren's hands that were hidden inside the pots.

For days Cole and I had been stumped on how to create realistic-looking flames. We'd tried half a dozen fabrics and hated them all, before we'd found it: red-gold satin. We'd cut the fabric into flamelike shapes, filled them with polyester toy stuffing, and sewn the flames together and onto the wicks.

We'd used satin again, gold this time, to create the

main body of the costume. Our first sketch had Darren walking in a pipe-shaped costume that would cover his legs and feet. Ms. Snow had critiqued our sketch and worried that our costume would make it difficult for Darren to move onstage. She suggested that Cole and I go to the theater and watch a rehearsal so we could see how much Darren moved when he danced and sang.

After we'd watched Darren go through his part, Cole and I gave each other The Look. The look of *I can't believe we almost made him wear that*! Darren was all over the stage, and our initial sketch would have been a huge pain to wear.

Cole and I redid the sketch with Darren in mind. This time we got the green light from Ms. Snow. We'd drawn a shirt with long gold sleeves and gold pants. As a final touch we'd added gold socks with rubber grips on the bottom. Darren would have much more freedom in pants than our original idea.

The rest of the costumes created by my class were amazing. Khloe looked stunning in every outfit. The rest of the costumes, from Chip to the Beast, were creative and interesting to look at onstage.

Now the work of my fashion class really showed while the entire cast was onstage.

Khloe, in the center of the stage, stepped forward from the rest of the cast. Her brown wig was piled and curled into an elegant half updo. Her final costume was a gleaming gold ball gown and white gloves. She looked like a princess! In Belle fashion, she curtsied and got a thunderous applause. Beaming Khloe stepped back in line, and Sam, who played the Beast, stepped forward for his moment in the spotlight. He received the same applause. Together the cast bowed, and I got teary. My best friend had nailed it.

It wasn't easy fighting the exiting crowd to get backstage. I carried Khloe's flowers in one arm and climbed down a few stairs. The excited, cheerful vibe was almost palpable. All of the actors were high-fiving each other or the crew. It was a scene full of smiles, and I grinned when I saw the brightest one.

"Khlo!" I called.

She'd taken off Belle's wig and gloves but was still in the gown. Khloe shot a hand into the air, waving at me, and I skirted around a few furry wolves to get to her.

"Congratulations!" I said. "You *killed* it!" I offered her the bouquet of flowers.

She covered her mouth with one hand before reaching

for them. "Lauren, oh my God. You didn't have to do that! This is so sweet!"

Khloe smelled the flowers and hugged me.

"Are you kidding me? I had to get you flowers. KK, I watched you work like *crazy* for this moment. You were the star of the play, and not because of the role. You brought this . . . this energy to the stage. I am so proud of you!"

Khloe Kinsella teared up in front of me. She never cried! I'd only seen her cry when we'd made up after a huge, awful fight.

"Laur," she said, shaking her head. "You have no idea what that means to me. I'm so happy that you think I did well. You're my best friend, and your opinion means so much."

"You did more than well. You did *amazing.*" I smiled. "I'm so happy I got my tickets for the rest of the week. Any idiots who didn't come tonight are going to be sorry, because there's going to be a riot on campus for tickets!"

Khloe laughed, shaking her head. "Oh, please."

"I think someone else might want to congratulate you," I said, looking over her shoulder.

"Who?" Khloe turned.

Zack walked up to Khloe, smiling at her. He had a dozen pink and red roses in his arms.

"I'm so lucky to be dating the girl who's going to be on Broadway one day," Zack said. He held the flowers out to Khloe, and she looked back at me, letting out a tiny squeal.

"I'll see you back at Hawthorne," I whispered to her, winking.

I left backstage with a smile on my face. Khloe had her very own real Prince Charming.

26

NOT ONCE
BUT TWICE

"OMIGOD, LAUREN, OMIGOD!" KHLOE YELLED.
We were getting dressed in our room for school.

"Shhhh!" I said. Khloe was on her computer, and knowing her, it was probably a breakup of the current A-list couple or some other celeb news. "Whatever it is, everyone in Hawthorne had to have heard you. Christina's probably going to be at our door in a second."

Khloe lowered her laptop lid shut, and I looked at her. Uh-oh.

This wasn't about Hollywood gossip. Khloe's usually tan face was a pasty white, and she looked as if she might be sick.

"Khloe." I got off my computer chair, taking the laptop off her lap, and settled beside her on Khloe's bed.

"I'm so sorry I said that. It's obviously much more serious. What's wrong?"

Khloe swallowed. She shook her head, seeming as if she was trying to clear her mind.

"Lauren, I'm so sorry to have to tell you this."

Now it was my turn to pale. I held my breath.

"He's okay now, but Mr. Conner broke his leg."

"What? How? Oh my God!"

My riding instructor seemed untouchable. Someone who could be kicked and walk away without a bruise. Someone who could handle any horse, no matter what the circumstances.

"He had taken the older advanced team—Sasha's group—on a cross-country ride this morning. Mr. Conner was riding Lexington, probably because he wanted to get him used to being in groups and unfamiliar territory."

"I can't believe it was a *riding* accident," I said in a whisper.

"I know. Mr. Conner, Sasha, and the other riders on her team had crossed the street to practice in a new field. I don't know all of the details—it's just an e-mail from this girl Alison Robb, who sent it out to everyone—but Lexington spooked and reared. He flipped onto his back."

I covered my mouth with my hand.

"Mr. Conner sustained a broken leg, but things could have been so much worse. Clearly."

"Do you know where he is now?"

"It sounded from Alison's email like she was writing from her BlackBerry in the hospital. Mr. Conner *was* okay enough to tell her to inform any riders—aka us—who have afternoon lessons that we're not to miss them. Mr. Conner won't be teaching, but Mike will be."

"Wow. *Oh, mon Dieu.*"

I sat still, almost unable to believe what I'd heard. I'd looked at Mr. Conner as someone who was invincible.

The rest of the morning was quiet as Khloe and I got ready and headed off to classes. I participated in English class, but my brain was thinking about the get-well card that I wanted to get Mr. Conner.

In the hall, my mouth may have been forming words talking to Taylor about his placement on the swim team and congratulating him, but my mind was on Mr. Conner. If a rider like that could take such a spill, when was it going to happen to one of us next?

At lunch Khloe and I slid into a table with Lexa and Clare. We picked at our food. Instead of forcing myself to eat, I pulled out a notebook, and with my Pilot pen I wrote down names of people to ask to sign Mr. Conner's get-well-soon card. It was a tiny gesture, but it was the gift we all agreed upon to give Mr. C.

After lunch Khloe and I went to study hall. Ms. Snow was supervising that day. We explained our situation and asked if we could be excused to go to the campus store, get a get-well card, and start collecting signatures. Ms. Snow couldn't have been any cooler about it. She expressed her sympathies for Mr. Conner and gave Khloe and me permission to do whatever we needed during the period. Ms. Snow even said that she wanted to sign the card.

At the day's end Khloe and I had a card full of signatures, and there wasn't a centimeter of white space left. We delivered it to the campus secretary, who promised to send it to Mr. Conner immediately.

Khloe and I left the administration building and started back to Hawthorne to change into our riding clothes.

"It's going to be so weird with Mike teaching," I said. "I know he's totally capable, but he's not Mr. Conner."

"It *is* going to be strange," Khloe agreed. "But think of Mr. Conner. He'd want us to pretend that he was teaching and have a great lesson."

I nodded. "You're definitely right about that."

"Guys, wait up!"

Khloe and I turned, and Clare hurried up the sidewalk behind us. We'd seen her earlier when we'd gotten her signature, and she'd been as shaken as all of us about what had happened.

"Hey, what's up?" I said.

"Yeah, you look all flushed in an excited way," Khloe said. "What's going on?"

"I *am* excited. I feel bad, though, feeling like that when Mr. Conner's in the hospital," Clare said.

"I'm sure he's on plenty of pain medication," I said. "Tell us what's going on!"

"Okay." Clare nodded. "You're probably right about the medication."

"Spill before my hair starts to go gray!" Khloe said, only half joking.

I grinned at the two friends when they stuck out their tongues at each other.

"I got *this* in my in-box this morning. Look." Clare thrust a piece of paper in front of us. It was dated as of yesterday and had been sent just after ten at night.

Subject: Your new roommate
Dear Ms. Bryant:

We, your housing coordinators at Canterwood Crest Academy, are writing to inform you that a new student will be moving into your room on the Saturday of Parents' Weekend. This student is a female transfer, and because it is late in the season for new students, we do not have time to set up an e-mail correspondence between the two of you.

We expect that you will welcome our new enrollee to Canterwood Crest and assist her with any help she may need.

If you have any questions, please feel free to stop by our office or reply to this e-mail.

Sincerely,
The Housing Coordinators of Canterwood

"How do you feel?" I asked.

"Yeah," Khloe said. "That's going to be a huge change for you, Clare-bear. You've only ever lived with, erm, Riley and then on your own."

"I'm actually really excited," Clare said. "It's been kind of lonely in my room since Riley ditched us. It'll be a new, good experience for me to live with someone else. She'll be getting here at a busy time, though, so I'll be out of my room a lot. But that might be good for her to get a feel of things on her own for a few hours instead of having me right there in her face."

"I'm happy for you," I said. "I can't wait to meet her."

27

NOT EVERYONE IS "FAMILY"

FRIDAY AFTERNOON THE CANTERWOOD PARK-ing lot was packed with students waiting for their parents to arrive.

"It's kind of funny," I said to Khloe. "Most of us are like, 'I'm *so* glad my parents aren't here hanging over me!' and then the second everyone gets a chance to see them, we all end up in the parking lot, like, an hour before they're scheduled to start arriving."

Khloe laughed. "I didn't think about that, but you're right. Look at all of us!"

We glanced around, giggling. Lexa and Clare sat together on the wooden fence a few feet away. Taylor and Matt, his roommate, stood with Zack and were animatedly talking about something.

Drew stood with Cole and some guys from the swim team. Plus, the seventh graders weren't the only ones who'd come to greet their parents. Plenty of older students had come out too.

Cars, SUVs, and vans started rolling up Canterwood's winding driveway. The activity excited the horses in the pastures on either side of the drive. One chestnut with a giant star on his head let out an ear-piercing whinny and started trotting along the fence, keeping pace with a black Escalade.

Car doors opened, students hurried to the open doors, and the driveway seemed like a safe zone. A what-happens-in-the-parking-lot-stays-in-the-parking-lot situation. A couple of girls in my math class whose parents arrived ran to their parents' cars and barely waited for their parents to get out before hugging them.

"Mom and Dad are here!" Khloe squealed. She pointed to a silver minivan. "There they are!" She waved and bounced up and down.

"Go, go!" I said, lightly pushing her.

With a huge grin Khloe jogged over to the minivan and stood by the passenger door. A blond woman, who looked *insanely* like Khloe, got out and threw her arms around her daughter. Khloe's dad, a sweet-looking guy in jeans and a polo shirt under a leather jacket, got out and hurried to his wife and daughter. The family three-way hugged, and I got a little teary watching them.

Then I heard a familiar engine. A *très* familiar black SUV rolled up to the parking lot. I saw Mom and Dad through the windshield and waved like crazy. I didn't care who saw me.

Mom and Dad waved back and pulled into one of the few open spots in the lot.

I ran across the grass and darted across the pavement covered in gravel.

"Mom! Dad!"

The SUV's engine went off, and my parents got out. They both hurried toward me and grabbed me in a giant hug and swung me around. The three of us laughed, and like I'd been starved for home, I smelled every scent that reminded me of our house. The hazelnut coffee Dad drank every morning before he started writing, the leather from Mom's briefcase, her Chanel No. 5 perfume, and just . . . home.

"LaurBell, you look amazing," Dad said. He cupped my face in his hands to get a better look.

"My little girl is actually being seen with her ancient parents out in public," Mom teased, hugging me tighter. "I can't remember the last time that happened."

"Oh, don't worry," I teased. "I'll ditch you guys later to make things normal again."

A car door opened and closed from our backseat, and Becca ran over to me.

"Omigod! I couldn't wait another second! I was trying to give you time with Mom and Dad, but that was all I could take!" My sister, my beautiful older sister that I loved more than anyone else in the world, wrapped her arms around me. Blond Becs looked nothing like me. She was only two years older, so we never went through the *I hate you* phase like many of my friends did with their sisters. We'd always been best friends.

My oldest sister, Charlotte, was the only one missing. She and I weren't exactly close, but we were working on it. Charlotte was away at college—Sarah Lawrence—and she hadn't been able to leave school to come to Canterwood. She promised she'd call me this weekend, though, and I believed her.

"I brought you a present," Becca said, grinning. "It's not anything big, so don't get excited."

"Becs! You didn't have to do that!" I said. "Thank you!"

"Help me get it out of the backseat?"

"Of course!"

I followed Becca around to the other side of the SUV and, through the slightly tinted window, saw something . . . *lumpy* covered with a green-and-gold Canterwood blanket.

"What—"

"SURPRISE!"

I jumped back, screaming.

"OH MY GOD! OH MY GOD!"

Sitting in the backseat, a newly blond Brielle grinned at me.

"Lauren!"

Brielle scrambled out of the backseat and landed on her feet. Her once-black-now-blond hair really complemented her complexion. She looked like the always chic Brielle in a navy long-sleeve sweater with an oatmeal-colored Fair Isle jacket belted around her waist. We threw our arms around each other and rocked as we hugged.

"How did you . . . And your parents . . . And my parents . . ." I couldn't finish a sentence.

We let go of each other, and I couldn't stop grinning. Neither could Brielle.

"I couldn't stay away from my LaurBell. So I promised my parents that I'd get As all semester if they let me come visit you. You know how much grades mean to them."

I nodded.

"Your parents were supercool and had no problem bringing me along. I'm not 'family' but I still got in."

I still couldn't believe I was staring at my best friend.

"This is one of the biggest surprises ever." I turned to Mom and Dad. "Thank you. Thank you so much!"

They nodded, smiling.

"You deserve it, sweetie," Dad said.

"Now we have to make sure none of the administration finds out who you are," I said to Bri. "If anyone asks, you're my cousin."

"I'm so not worried about it," Brielle said.

"Ah! I have so much to show you guys! Want to see Whisper?"

"Today's *your* day," Mom said. "You show us everything you want. You're in charge."

"I like the sound of that."

Everyone laughed.

With that, I began a tour of Canterwood that showed my family and Brielle *everything* that I loved about my school.

During the hours I spent showing them my English classroom and getting them to the auditorium on time for my glee club performance, I didn't see any of my Canterwood friends, Taylor, or Drew. Everyone was absorbed in their own families. It felt like that was exactly the way it should be.

28

FACE-OFF

"I CAN'T WAIT TO BE HOME FOR THANKSGIVING break," I said to my parents and Becca. It was already Saturday afternoon, and time for all the parents to leave. Mine had spent the night at a nearby hotel, and Bri and Becca had shared an adjoining room.

The three of us were walking back to the parking lot. It was time for my family and Bri to leave. Bri had forgotten her phone in my room and had run back to get it before she left with Mom, Dad, and Becca. The sun was nearly set. I couldn't believe how fast the day had gone by.

"We can't wait to have you home, honey," Mom said. "Thanksgiving break is so short. Dad and I were already talking about how much we're looking forward to your Christmas vacation."

The thought made me smile. "A longer break doesn't exactly make me sad," I said. "Finals will be over, and I get to come home to holiday tea, and fires, and presents."

"Jeez, what about coming home to your dear old dad?" Dad asked, winking at me.

I rolled my eyes to the sky and pretended to think. "Hmmm. I *guess* seeing you, Mom, Becs, and Char won't be awful or anything."

Laughing, Dad slung an arm across my shoulders. "That's my LaurBell."

I started to reply, but two people in the distance caught my eye. Next to the parking lot, Taylor and Brielle stood in front of one another. Brielle gestured with her arms, and her cheeks were pink. Taylor's arms were crossed, and he shook his head. As we got closer, I saw his clenched jaw and his tense body language.

". . . you can't . . . anything," Brielle snapped at him.

I nudged Becca's arm with my elbow to get her attention, but she was already watching what I wanted her to see.

". . . don't . . . unfair," Taylor said. His voice was too low for me to make out more than two words.

I broke away from my family and headed toward my friends. Before I could reach them, Taylor glared at Brielle and walked off in the opposite direction.

Brielle shook her head, seeming to try to shake off whatever had happened. She looked up, probably at the sound of my shoes crunching on the gravel.

"Hey," Bri said as she walked toward me.

"What *was* that?" I asked, stopping in front of her. I didn't care that cars were edging around us as we stood in the middle of the busy parking lot.

Brielle rolled her eyes and sighed. "Boys. Taylor ran into me when I was leaving your dorm, and he wanted to talk about something. I told him I had to meet you and we could talk about it later."

A white Suburban backed up next to us, and a blond woman motioned for us to step out of the way.

Brielle and I moved a few paces back, but I didn't take my eyes off her face. She looked shaken, and Bri *never* got scared.

"Did Taylor follow you down here?" I asked. "Or was he coming to say good-bye to his parents?"

"The Frosty Freezes?" Brielle referenced them by the nickname Ana had given Mr. and Mrs. Frost when we'd first met them. She shook her head. "No. They left, like, an hour ago, Taylor said. But I thought the same thing at first— that Taylor was coming to the parking lot to see them. But he told me he was following me to your parents' SUV."

This was *not* the Taylor I knew.

"I can't believe it. I mean, there's been a little *something* off with Taylor since he got here. But nothing that would make him act like that. What did he want to talk about? What was such a big deal?"

Bri looked down at her caramel-colored boots. "I did something dumb a couple of months ago. It happened and Taylor froze me out until he left Yates for Canterwood. I said I was sorry on the phone, but apparently that wasn't enough."

"Brielle. What? Tell me." I couldn't decide if I wanted to shake the answer out of her or hug her.

"Lauren, I feel so bad." Brielle sniffled, and she wrapped her arms across her chest. "A couple of days after you left for Canterwood, Taylor, Ana, and I were supposed to go to the movies."

"Okay . . ."

Brielle took a ragged breath. "Taylor was supposed to be at his dad's office that day, but he told Mr. Frost that he was sick so he could go out with Ana and me. Mrs. Frost was off having a spa day, so my mom and I were supposed to pick him up, and Mom was going to drop us at the mall to meet Ana."

The volume of voices in the parking lot and the sounds

of engines started to fade as more and more parents left Canterwood. I looked across the lot, and Mom, Dad, and Becca waited patiently by our SUV. I held up a finger in the *give me one minute* gesture. Dad nodded and he, Mom, and Becca climbed inside to wait for Brielle.

"About an hour before it was time to pick up Taylor, I got sick for real," Bri said. "I threw up and got the chills." She snapped her fingers. "It happened just like that. I couldn't go, but I still wanted him to see the movie with Ana. Plus, I had to let him know I wasn't coming. I tried his cell, and it kept going to voice mail. I left him a bunch of messages before I started getting worried that he'd miss the movie because he wouldn't know that my mom couldn't pick him up because she had to take care of me."

"Wait. *Wait.* You're not going to tell me that Taylor was that upset because he missed a movie, are you?"

Brielle shook her head. A cold breeze blew leaves across the parking lot. I shivered, zipping up my jacket.

"I wish. I thought he was home alone, and I wasn't getting through on his cell. He'd told Ana and me that his mom wouldn't be back until after dinner and same for his dad. So I called his home number. It rang and rang, and the answering machine picked up. I told him that I was sick and he needed to call Ana or he'd miss the movie."

A sick feeling lurched in my stomach. I knew what Brielle was going to say. I just knew it.

"I was two seconds away from hanging up, and mid-sentence someone picked up the phone," Bri said. She rubbed her forehead with her hand. "Mr. Frost. He asked me how it was possible that his son was going to the movies, because he was sick in bed."

"Oh God."

"I know. Lauren, I tried to fix it! I told Mr. Frost that I knew Taylor was very sick and we'd gotten in a fight a few days ago. I lied and said I was trying to make Tay feel bad that Ana and I were going to the movies and was throwing it in his face that he could have come if he just called Ana for a ride."

I groaned. "Mr. Frost didn't buy it." Now I rubbed my forehead with my hand. A headache started to form behind my eyes.

"He didn't say anything after I finished talking," Brielle said. "Just 'Thank you, Brielle,' and he hung up. Days went by, and Ana and I didn't hear from Taylor. When we finally did, he instant messaged me that his dad had come home because he'd forgotten something and figured out Taylor was faking being sick when he heard me on the answering machine."

"Poor Taylor," I said, groaning.

Brielle nodded, her brown eyes teary. She tucked a lock of blond hair behind her ear. "Taylor said he got in so much trouble that I almost ruined his chance at coming to Canterwood. I felt sick about it, Laur. I really did apologize a million times, but Taylor wouldn't talk to me until today."

I let out a huge breath. "Wow. I'm so sorry for both of you. Bri, of course you felt bad, but you made a mistake. I know you apologized a zillion times—that's who you are. I understand Taylor's side too, if he was still angry and wanted to talk it out in person, but he *never* should have come after you like that. Are you okay?"

I reached out my arms and hugged my friend.

Brielle nodded into my shoulder. "Yeah, I'm fine. I feel bad all over again."

I let her go but squeezed her hand. "You've felt bad long enough, Bri. You've apologized and that's all you can do. I'm sorry that Taylor got in trouble, but he *did* end up here. He was a jerk to blow up at you."

Brielle shrugged. "It's okay. I'm glad he got it off his chest, and I really don't want to talk to him for a while."

"You won't have to," I reassured her. "You'll be at home

and he'll be here. And you can bet I'm going to talk to Taylor about what happened today."

I motioned toward my parents' direction with a head tilt. "The timing's really awful, but I need to go say good-bye. Mom and Dad have been cool about waiting."

Brielle nodded. "Don't worry about it. Your parents *have* been awesome."

She followed me to the SUV and stood near the back-seat, where she'd sit next to Becca on the ride back to Union.

Mom, Dad, and Becca got out of the warm vehicle and took turns hugging me. Mom and Dad knew better than to ask me what had just happened with my friends. Becca, however, mouthed *talk later,* and I nodded at her.

"I love you," I said to Dad. He kissed the top of my head.

"You're my girl, Laur. I love you and we'll see you soon," Dad said. I hugged him a second longer, taking in the feeling of his arms around me. I missed him more than I'd ever admit—more than I ever thought I would.

"Bye, Mom," I said. We hugged and exchanged I-love-yous before she got back in the SUV with Dad, leaving me with Becca and Brielle.

"C'mere, LaurBell," Becs said. My sister wrapped her

arms around me. Her hug felt loving, protective, and big sisterly all at once. "BBM you when we get home, 'kay?"

I nodded. I didn't want Becca to leave. My older sister was one of my best friends. I missed her every single day and still wasn't used to being away from her.

"I miss you," I said, holding back tears.

"Me too. But you're coming home really soon. We'll hang out so much that you'll be like, 'Oh my God. I can't wait to get away from annoying Becca and get back to school!'"

"No, I won't," I said, smiling at her.

"Mwah," Becca said, blowing me a kiss as she got into the backseat.

I turned to Brielle. "I hate saying good-bye," I said. "I miss seeing you every day."

Bri smiled. "I hate good-byes too. Not seeing you in the Yates halls was really weird."

"Was?" I made a pretend-offended face. "So you're used to it and over not seeing me around anymore?"

Bri shook her head. "No way. I said 'was' because it really won't be weird anymore."

"Why?" I tilted my head.

Bri smiled. "Well . . . because I won't be walking the Yates halls anymore. Oh, and you're not going to have to say another good-bye."

I stood in the parking lot. Just stood there and stared at her. My brain must have been fried from Parents' Weekend activity overload, because I had *no* idea what Brielle was saying. The family dinner, the sitting in on classes at weird times, and the teachers I'd introduced my parents to must have made me more tired than I'd realized.

"I don't get it." I shook my head.

Brielle's smile turned into an ear-to-ear grin. "Let's see if I can say it more clearly. You don't have to say good-bye to me. I won't be in the halls at Yates because I'm going to be in the halls at Canterwood." Bri reached out and squeezed my forearms. "Lauren, I got accepted to Canterwood as a midseason transfer!"

"What?" It felt like the cold air had snatched away my breath.

"I'm serious!" Bri let go of me and bounced on her toes. "*This* is really the big surprise! Your parents and Becca are in on it too! They brought me like I was coming to visit you, but they were really dropping me off. I'll explain all of the deets to you when we're not outside freezing, but I'm staying!"

"Omigod! Omigod!" I squealed and mimicked Bri's bounce.

This was insane.

This was almost incomprehensible.

This didn't feel real.

Taylor wasn't even settled in yet, and now I had a second friend from home at my school. Brielle was more than a friend—she was one of my best friends.

"And guess who's Clare's new roommate?"

"No. Way."

My brain felt as though it was going to explode from shock and excitement. Barely two minutes ago I'd been steeling myself to say good-bye to one of my best friends who had surprised me by visiting. Now Bri *shocked* me by revealing that she wasn't climbing in the SUV with my family.

Brielle wasn't a Yates student.

Brielle was a Canterwood Crest student.

This was going to change *everything*.

Bri grabbed me in a giant hug. "Now your bestie from home is here!"

ABOUT THE AUTHOR

Twenty-five-year-old Jessica Burkhart (a.k.a. Jess Ashley) writes from Brooklyn, New York. She's obsessed with sparkly things, lip gloss, and TV. She loves hanging with her bestie, watching too much TV, and shopping for all things Hello Kitty. Learn more about Jess at www.JessicaBurkhart.com. Find everything Canterwood Crest at www.CanterwoodCrest.com.